William Westall

Her two millions

Vol. I

William Westall

Her two millions
Vol. I

ISBN/EAN: 9783743377134

Manufactured in Europe, USA, Canada, Australia, Japa

Cover: Foto ©Andreas Hilbeck / pixelio.de

Manufactured and distributed by brebook publishing software (www.brebook.com)

William Westall

Her two millions

HER TWO MILLIONS.

BY

WILLIAM WESTALL,

Author of

" Red Ryvington," " The Phantom City," " Two Pinches of
Snuff," etc.

IN THREE VOLUMES.

VOL. I.

LONDON:

WARD AND DOWNEY,

12, YORK STREET, COVENT GARDEN, W.C.
1887.

PRINTED BY
KELLY AND CO., GATE STREET, LINCOLN'S INN FIELDS,
AND KINGSTON-ON-THAMES

CONTENTS.

HER TWO MILLIONS.

ONE-VOLUME NOVELS.

———◆———

A TERRIBLE LEGACY. By G. W. APPLETON. 6s.

JACK ALLYN'S FRIENDS. By G. W. APPLETON. 3s. 6d.

TWO PINCHES OF SNUFF. By WILLIAM WESTALL. 3s. 6d.

A BIRD OF PASSAGE. By B. M. CROKER. 6s.

IN ONE TOWN. By E. DOWNEY. 3s. 6d.

ANCHOR WATCH YARNS. By E. DOWNEY. 3s. 6d.

A HOUSE OF TEARS. By E. DOWNEY. 1s.

A MENTAL STRUGGLE. By the Author of " MOLLY BAWN." 6s.

THE MASTER OF THE CEREMONIES. By G. M. FENN. 6s.

WARD & DOWNEY, PUBLISHERS, LONDON.

HER TWO MILLIONS.

CHAPTER I.

IT is past midnight. A serene moon, set in a purple sky, shines over the Lago Maggiore, crowning with a golden aureole the snow-crested peaks of the Helvetic Alps, and beaming benignly on the towers of Locarno and the shores of the Lake. But Locarno sleeps, the streets are deserted, and a small boat, which follows swiftly in the wake of the moonbeams, approaches the jetty unperceived. It contains four men; two are rowing, the third is steering and minding the sail; the fourth lies huddled up in the bottom of the boat, his bandaged head resting on a cushion, his pale face streaked with blood.

When his companions, all of whom wear red shirts, have made fast the boat to the jetty, they lift him tenderly out, and two, placing themselves on either side of their wounded comrade, half lead, half carry him to an inn a few hundred paces from the landing place. The doors are closed and all is silent within, but a strong pull at the bell brings a head speedily to one of the upper windows.

"Who is there?"

"We, and Leonino is hurt. Come down and open quickly."

The next moment the doors are thrown open and a stout little man, with nothing much on save a white shirt, appears at the threshold in a state of great excitement.

"Dreadful, dreadful!" he exclaims. "Poor Signor Leonino, is he much hurt? How did it happen? I knew it would come to this at last. Yet better so than that he should fall into the hands of those thrice accursed Tedeschi. But tell me how it happened afterwards. Let us get him up-stairs at once. And here, Maximilano (shouting), fetch the doctor immediately. Go, running; tell Dr. Fadio to come quickly. I hope you are not in pain, dear Leonino. You can walk just a little—a very little —and we will support you up-stairs."

"I can get one leg before the other, if that is what you mean, Martino," gasps Leonino. "But stand I cannot. Yes, I shall be glad to get to my room and lie down. My head pains me terribly, and that bullet in my shoulder burns like fire. I shall never get over this, Giacomo."

"Don't say that, Signor," says one of the red-shirted ones. "Dr. Fadio shall dress your wounds, and in a month you will be as strong as ever. Come, now, lean on me, put one arm round Umberto's neck—thus, and we will carry you to your room. It is not far off. Courage, steady now!"

The room to which they took him was on the first floor, large, airy, well lighted, and handsomely furnished. In one corner stood a bed on which Leonino was laid. The man whom he had called Martino, the keeper of the inn, took off his shoes and was proceeding to undress him.

"Don't," murmured Leonino. "I feel very much exhausted, let me rest a few minutes."

At this moment a woman *en déshabille*, and with a scared face, glided into the room.

"*Mon dieu! mon dieu!*" she exclaimed in an intense whisper. "What is this which has taken place? My poor patron! Is he killed?"

"Not at all," answered Giacomo sharply. "Dr. Fadio will soon put him to rights. But had you not better go? The less he is disturbed just now the better—and see, he sleeps."

"Is that Gabrielle?" asked Leonino feebly, opening his eyes.

"Yes, monsieur, it is I, Gabrielle."

"Vera!"

"She is quite well and very happy. She is in bed; shall I bring her?"

"My poor Vera! Yes, bring her. But stay, it is a pity to wake the child."

" Do not bring anybody at present, if you please, mademoiselle. Bring rather sponges, hot water, and towels. When I have dressed monsieur's wounds then he may perhaps see his daughter." This in French.

The speaker was Dr. Fadio, a tall, middle-aged gentleman, leathern-skinned and lantern-jawed, with bright black eyes and a pleasant smile. He was an old army surgeon, and without more ado he began, deftly and tenderly, to examine his patient's wounds.

Gabrielle and Martino stood by to help him. The one held a lamp, the other a basin of water. Near the window, and in the light of the moon, stood the three red-shirted men, with folded arms, looking sadly and sternly on. They were pale, seemed almost overcome with fatigue, and the head of one and the arm of another were bandaged, as if they too had been wounded.

The wound in Leonino's head was long and deep, and as the doctor examined it his face grew very grave. When the hurt had been stitched and plastered he extracted the bullet which was lodged in the shoulder, an operation that did not appear to be attended with any great difficulty.

" Who will watch with him ? " asked Fadio in Italian, when all was finished.

" I will," said Gabrielle and Martino. " We will," chorused the red shirts.

"Nonsense," answered the doctor, "you three are fit for nothing but bed. What is the matter with your head, Umberto? I must see to it presently. Let Gabrielle watch. I shall return at sunrise."

Whereupon Fadio beckoned them all to leave the room, and after giving a few directions to Gabrielle, and casting a last look at his patient, he followed them.

"Well, Signor Doctor, what do you think?" asked Martino, drawing him into a room near the foot of the staircase. "Can you pull him through?"

"I am not sure. He is very badly hurt; still, neither of his wounds is mortal, and if he had not lost so much blood I should have little fear. The question is whether he can rally. A few hours will tell. How was it, Giacomo? Another brush with the Austrians?"

"Si, Signor Dottore. It was an attempt to rescue Silvio."

"A rash undertaking."

"True; but he and Leonino are great friends, and Leonino risked his life to save a friend, as he has done many a time before. Pietri went in disguise the other day to Laverco, and contrived to communicate with Silvio and convey to him a file and some cord. It was arranged that he should make the attempt last night. We were to be there with

the boat, and ready to give him a helping hand if
he should be pursued by the guard. That was the
chief risk, for with a file and a cord anybody could
get out of the fort. But the night was too light.
Silvio was seen before he had got well out of the
dry ditch, followed and recaptured. We tried to
rescue him; shots were exchanged; Beppo was
killed, Leonino wounded, as you see, and all of us
are in want of a little plaister, I think."

"Good; I will plaister you, and then you must
each take a glass of wine and go to bed. Yes, a
rash undertaking indeed. The idea of five Red
Shirts trying to carry off a prisoner under the very
noses of an Austrian demi-brigade! Nobody but
Garibaldi—or a mad Englishman—would have had
the audacity to concoct such a scheme, much less to
execute it. The wonder is, you were not all killed
or taken."

"We were beaten; but we made them pay dearly,"
broke in Giacomo fiercely. "We killed four; Leonino ran the sergeant of the guard through, just as
he got that cut on the head. If it had not been
for that we should have been taken. But the
sergeant's death seemed to confuse his men, and we
profited by their hesitation to shove off. The bullet
in Leonino's shoulder was a parting shot. Fortunately nobody else was hit, or we should not be here.
The soldiers did get a boat out and chase us; but
we ran close to the bank, under the shade of

some trees, and they shot past us. Leonino is a fine
fellow, doctor, and a true friend to Italy. It would
be a thousand pities if he were to die."

"I will do my best to keep him alive, Giacomo,
both for the sake of Italy and that dear little dark-
eyed Vera. But man proposes and God disposes,
and Leonino is badly hurt and very weak."

CHAPTER II.

A DEPARTURE.

THREE hours later Dr. Fadio was again with his patient.

" Has he slept ? " he asked Gabrielle, who sat by the bedside.

" A little," said Leonino, opening his eyes. He was a man in the prime of life, with blue eyes, tawny hair and beard, and a bold, handsome face, but its general expression was that of one who is oppressed with care or cherishes the memory of a great sorrow.

" And how do you feel ? "

A wistful smile was the answer.

" Not very well, I am afraid ? "

" Very ill, I never felt like this before. I have got my death-stroke. Poor Vera! no mother, no father."

The doctor counted his patient s pulse and watched him attentively several minutes.

"He must have a little beef-tea every hour, Gabrielle, and when he feels faint give him a spoonful of cognac."

"*Oui, monsieur.*"

"Vera; may I see Vera?"

"Yes, if you will not let yourself get excited; but only for a few minutes. You can fetch her, Gabrielle, I will wait."

In a few minutes Gabrielle returned, leading by the hand a little girl of some seven years old. The child had a wonderfully sweet face, and though her eyes were dark, her curls were chestnut, and she bore a striking resemblance to Leonino.

A smile of deepest love lit up the father's face.

"Darling Vera!" he said. "Lift her up on the bed, Gabrielle; place her near me."

"We will leave you together for a few minutes," said the doctor, glancing at the nurse, and then the two went out of the room.

"Are you ill, papa dear?" asked the child in English, as she nestled up to her father, and placed her cheek against his.

"Very ill, darling," answered Leonino in the same tongue; "I have been badly hurt."

"Hurt! Oh, dear! Who hurt you?"

"The Austrians."

"Those wicked Austrians! How I hate them! Why does not somebody kill them all? Why don't you kill them, papa?"

"That is not so easy, my pet. I am afraid they have killed me this time."

"No, no, no, papa! It is not possible. You must not die. If you die, Vera will die, too."

"I will do my best to live for your sake, darling. But it may be a long time before I am better—and if—Gabrielle will take care of you. She is a good woman, and I think loves you, and you love her, do you not?"

"Yes, dear papa, next to you; but a long, long way after. I have nobody like you, dear papa."

"Well, she shall be your *bonne* always, if she will, and I think she will. How would you like to go to your grandpapa?"

"No, no; I never saw him. I love no one like you, dear papa. Let me stay with you always—always."

"God Almighty bless you, my darling! and may the pure spirit of your mother watch over you!" murmured Leonino in a broken voice. And then he drew the child closer to him, and there followed a long silence.

When the doctor and Gabrielle re-entered the room Vera was fast asleep, and Leonino's eyes being closed, he too seemed to sleep. They made a striking picture. The child's bright, rosy face touched one of her father's pale and hollow cheeks, her chestnut hair mingled with his tawny beard, one dimpled arm was round his neck, one little hand was pressed in his.

"Let us leave them for a little while," whispered Fadio. "No harm is being done. But prepare the beef-tea. He does not rally much, and unless we keep up his strength he will sink."

In half an hour they returned, and at the doctor's suggestion Leonino reluctantly allowed the child to be taken away to her breakfast.

"But you will let me see her again?" he said imploringly.

"Certainly, when you have taken your beef-tea and rested awhile. I want you to sleep; there is no medicine like sleep."

The beef-tea taken, Leonino sank wearily on his pillow, shut his eyes, and tried to sleep, and the doctor left him for a while to Gabrielle.

After an hour's uneasy slumber Leonino awoke.

"Gabrielle!"

"*Oui, monsieur*. How do you feel yourself?"

"Bad. Give me a taste of that brandy. Ah, that gives one a little strength; but it won't last long, I fear. I have something to say to you, Gabrielle."

"*Oui, monsieur*."

"You love Vera?"

"As if she were my very own. Have I not brought her up? Since her poor mother died has she not been everything to me?"

"And you will be kind to her?"

"Oh, monsieur!" said the *bonne* in an injured

tone, "how can you ask? It is doing me a
wrong."

"Well, listen. I don't feel as if I should get
better, and I judge from the doctor's manner that
he thinks as I feel. I have made no will; but I
shall write a few lines to my father, asking him to
take charge of Vera, and that you and she may
never be separated. You will take this letter and
the child to London, first writing to tell my father
what has happened. . . . . You are paying
attention, Gabrielle?"

"*Oui, monsieur*," said the *bonne*, wiping her
eyes, which were red with weeping.

"My father is a hard man; but he will be good
to you and Vera for my sake. I have made no will,
and shall make none; but, to prevent the authori-
ties troubling you afterwards, I will give into your
possession now all my money and papers. If I
should get better you can give me them back.
Open my trunk; you will find the keys in my
pocket."

Gabrielle took the keys and unlocked a large iron-
bound trunk, which stood in one corner of the room.

"Bring my portfolio and the little iron box,
which you will find at the bottom, right under my
clothes," said Leonino.

Gabrielle took these two articles, laid them on
the table near her master's bed, and at his request
brought writing materials and sealing-wax.

Then Leonino, sitting up in bed, wrote a letter to his father, enclosed with it several papers, made the whole up into a packet, and sealed it carefully with his signet ring.

"These," he said, taking a packet from the portfolio, "are letters from Garibaldi, Mazzini, and other friends engaged in the revolutionary movement. Destroy them all. But these " (pointing to a second packet) "are family papers of importance. Be sure you give them all to my father. You may also find a few bank-notes in the portfolio. I have always been careless about money— perhaps that is the reason I was never robbed. In the little iron box is also money, both gold and notes—several thousand liras, I think; never mind counting it now. If I don't get better you will, of course, pay Martino and the doctor, and everybody else, and you must give the men who were with me, Giacomo, Guiseppe, and Umberto, each two hundred and fifty liras. Then, after paying your expenses to England and taking five hundred liras as a present for yourself, you will give what there is left to my father, together with the packet. Give it to him with your own hands. Do you understand, Gabrielle ? "

" Perfectly. But pardon me, sir, don't you think this should be put down? It is a serious charge. Suppose anybody should say that you did not give me this money, that I stole it ! "

"I have thought of that. We must have a witness. Call Martino; but first give me another spoonful of cognac, I feel faint again."

When Martino came Leonino explained to him what he had done.

"It is better so," said the landlord; "all the same I think you will recover; but should you not, I can testify that you gave Mademoiselle Gabrielle this portfolio and this iron box."

"And the big box and all there is inside, Martino, I give to you, and this watch. It is not a very valuable one, but it has accompained me in all my wanderings and may serve to remind you sometimes of your old friend."

Martino, who was an Italian refugee and deeply engaged in the revolutionary movement, silently pressed Leonino's hand. He was too much affected to speak.

"My wife's watch, Gabrielle," said Leonino, after a short pause, "her miniature and mine you will keep for Vera and give them to her when—when she is older."

Gabrielle bent her head in token of assent.

"Poor Vera, poor child! I am trusting you with all that is most precious to me, Gabrielle, but you are a good woman; you will be faithful to your trust, and Vera will not be ungrateful. And—and —tell my father how I died, and give him my love. We did not always get on very well together, but he is an old man, and this will be a great shock to him."

A few minutes later Dr. Fadio came. When he had examined his patient he looked concerned.

"You have been letting him talk too much," he said, turning to Gabrielle. "Did I not tell you——"

"Don't blame her," interrupted Leonino wearily, "it is all my own doing. I do not know whether I shall live, and I had instructions to give her and something—a mere trifle—to write."

"You have actually been writing! The worst thing you could do."

"Never mind, doctor; my mind is easier now, and that must be better for my body, you know, and I promise you that I will sin no more."

"If you do I shall not answer for the consequences. And now, Gabrielle, we must dress his wounds."

When this was done Leonino asked if Vera might come to him again.

"You need not be afraid," he remarked, seeing that Fadio hesitated; "her presence does not excite, it soothes me."

"Very well, let her come. But except for a word or two now and then when you want something, I must absolutely forbid talking. See that he obeys, Mademoiselle Gabrielle, quietness is essential."

"Don't fear, doctor," said Leonino, with a melancholy smile, " you may count on my obedience. I shall be quiet enough, soon."

Fadio glanced at Gabrielle, and she went with him to the door.

"I fear he is worse—decidedly weaker," he whispered. "You should not quit his bedside without leaving somebody in your place. You had better" (raising his voice) "fetch Mademoiselle Vera at once. I will wait until you return."

In a few minutes the *bonne* returned with the child, who crept to the old place by her father's side. Leonino looked at her lovingly, put his arm round her and laid her face close to his. Gabrielle told her little charge that papa's head ached and she must not talk, and then sat down. The *bonne* was tired with watching and heavy with loss of rest ; before long her eyelids closed with their own weight, and she sank into a sound sleep.

A few moments afterwards, as it seemed to her, though in reality two or three hours, she was roused by a touch on the shoulder; looking up she saw the dark face of Dr. Fadio.

"A nurse should not slumber at her post," he said sternly. "Take the child away."

Vera was sleeping by her father's side, and the father slept the sleep of death.

The nurse gently disengaged the girl from the dead man's grasp, and took her into her arms.

"Come with me, *ma fille chérie*, papa is tired."

"Yes, Gabrielle, but I must first kiss him. Do let me kiss him." And then the child pressed her warm and rosy mouth to the cold and pallid cheek of her once father. She raised her head with a look of affright. "Oh, what is it?" she gasped; "what is it? He does not look at me—he is cold—he does not open his eyes! Papa! papa! Oh, Gabrielle, he does not speak to me, and his mouth is open!"

"Come with me, my poor motherless darling; your father will never speak again. You have only me now. Oh, my poor master! he was so good, so good to everybody, and everybody loved him."

CHAPTER III.

THREE days later Leonino was buried. All the Italian exiles in Locarno and many of the townsfolk followed his body to the grave, for though not Italian born, he had fought and bled in the cause of Italian liberty, and lost his life in a bold attempt to free from his bonds one of the most eminent of Italian patriots.

Gabrielle carried out faithfully her late master's wishes—saw him buried, discharged all his debts, and paid the two hundred and fifty liras apiece to Leonino's three companions in the unfortunate expedition to Laverco. She was making preparations for departure, and meant, a day or two after the funeral, to leave by the diligence for Fluelen, *en route* for England. As yet, however, she had not written to apprise Leonino's father of his son's death. She had been too much occupied; and the disposal of the money she had found in the portfolio and the cash-box gave her great concern. There were many bank-notes in the portfolio, mixed up with sundry political papers, whose existence Leonino had apparently forgotten. The sum in her hands was large. To her, who reckoned in francs and liras it seemed enormous. She did not know how she should secure it on the journey, and was in mortal terror of being robbed. Had she consulted Martino he would probably have advised her to buy a draft on London or Paris; but she was peasant-bred, and having all a peasant's shrewdness and distrust, kept her own counsel, and even told the landlord that the disposable balance, after all had been paid, was not very much. After much cogitation she hit upon the ingenious device of stitching the bank-notes inside her stays and putting the gold into her boots, which she hid among her clothes, and placed in the very bottom of her trunk.

This done she proceeded to write to Leonino's father. Gabrielle was a young woman of fair education, rather a nursery governess than an ordinary nurse, and she spoke English fairly. But speaking is one thing, writing quite another, and the framing of the letter cost her both time and trouble. She had hardly finished and addressed it when a letter was brought to her. It was rudely sealed, and the direction was written in a large, sprawling hand, but it bore a post-mark Gabrielle well knew, and she opened it with a feeling made up of pleasurable expectation and self-reproach, for it was a long time since she last wrote to her people.

2*

The letter was long, and as she read it her face grew graver and graver. The tidings it brought occupied her mind to the exclusion of everything else, and the letter to Mr. Hardy was never finished.

She was roused from her reverie by the entrance of Vera, who, like herself, wore deep mourning. The child's pale face and the dark circles round her eyes showed how sorely she grieved for her dead father. Throwing her arms round Gabrielle's neck, she sobbed as if her little heart would break. The *bonne* took the child on her lap and soothed her.

"When are we going, Gabrielle?" she said as soon as she could speak. "It is dreadful here now poor papa is gone. I went past his room just now; they are taking out all the things, and he is not there—he is not there! Oh, Gabrielle, my heart is breaking! Let us go! let us go!"

"We will go to-morrow. I did not think of leaving until Thursday; but it will perhaps be better to start to-morrow. Come with me to the post-office, and we will take our places. The walk will do us both good."

Martino and several other of Leonino's friends saw them off.

"You will write from London," said the landlord, as he wrung Gabrielle's hand, "and tell us of your safe arrival? It is rather a long journey; but you have travelled before, and are quite able to take care of yourself and the little one. If you should ever need a friend do not forget that Andrea Martino holds all that he has at the disposal of Leonino's daughter. *Bon voyage.*"

And then, amid a babel of stamping horses, cracking whips, tinkling bells, and shouting stablemen, the huge diligence, with Gabrielle and Vera weeping in the *coupé,* moved off towards Bellinzona.

"I shall never see them again," muttered Martino, as he walked with sad eyes towards his house. "Poor Leonino ! poor little girl ! "

CHAPTER IV.

A MEETING in the club-room of the "Cock," in the town of Calder.

The inn was old, and—though an attempt had been made to modernise it by substituting plate-glass windows for the more picturesque if less light-giving diamond-shaped panes of other days—so was the room. The ceiling was low, and ribbed with oaken rafters, the oaken door black with age, and there were oaken settles and chairs that a collector would have been glad to buy with money and fair words. Many a feast and dance and merrymaking has there been in the old club-room; its rafters have rung with the shouts and songs and laughter of many generations of roystering Calderites; and as much drink has been "consumed on the premises," as would float a fleet of ironclads. But the present meeting, as the absence of glasses testifies, is not of a festive character. Neither is it a meeting of creditors, nor of pothouse politicians, nor of any local society; and being held in a public-house it cannot

well be either a religious assembly or a teetotal
gathering. The people present number about a
score and a half, and among them are all sorts and
conditions of men — and women.

The chairman is a portly, well-dressed, well-fed
personage of some sixty years old. His fat, clean-
shaven face wears a stereotyped smile; his little
eyes are sharp and deep-set, and his head is fixed in
an enormous black stock, from which it seems to
have recently emerged. He carries his watch in a
fob, and sports a heavy chain and a still heavier
seal. Whatever else he may be this gentleman is
evidently well-to-do, and knows it. Not far from
him is a man the cut and appearance of whose
garments proclaim him a calico-weaver. Among the
others are a shoemaker, a blacksmith, a waggoner, a
butcher, a baker, several farmers, and three or four
women, one of whom carries a market-basket, and
is probably a farmer's wife.

"I don't know as I am called upon to make any
particular remarks," said the president without
rising from his chair. "You all know what has
brought us here, so I think as the best thing as I
can do is to call on Mr. Ferret to explain it, and
tell you what he advises about this 'ere fortune."

The individual thus addressed was a broad-set,
swarthy little man, with a thick nose and heavy
chaps, and a look more suggestive of a bull-dog
than of the animal whose name he bore.

"I think you are all Hardys?" said the lawyer — for such he was—as he rose to his feet.

"Or akin to 'em," answered the chairman, "except you and your clerk, and Mr. Balmaine here. We must keep friends with the press, you know; and he'll print nowt without showing it to me and Mr. Ferret."

"What good will that do?" put in the calico-weaver; "th' job will be done then."

"Publish, I should say; he'll publish nowt as we don't sanction."

"Aye, that's summat like. Yo' speyk when your mouth oppens, Mr. Hardy."

"Will you please go on, Mr. Ferret," said the chairman tartly. "These—these interruptions are unseemly."

"I am quite ready, Mr. Hardy," began the lawyer, who spoke fluently and easily, though in rather Yorkshire English. "You all know, I think, as I was the first to find out that the Hardys of this neighbourhood are probably entitled—in my opinion certainly entitled—to a very large fortune. I cannot say exactly how much, for them as has it in hand are very close, but it cannot be far short of two millions of money."

"By gum, that's a corker!" broke in the calico-weaver.

"Order!" exclaimed the chairman. "Really,

Tommy, you are behaving very badly. Will you please go on, Mr. Ferret."

" I say two millions at least," continued Ferret. " Why, John Hardy's personalty was sworn under £800,000; he had lots of land in the most improving parts of London, and then there's ten years' accumulations. Well, as I was going to say —for it's best to begin at the beginning—John Hardy died ten years since, and left all his estate, both real and personal, to his only son Philip—to his only child, I should say, for he had no other. Well, it has never been claimed, and I do not believe ever will be claimed, for we may be quite sure as if he was living two millions would fetch him; and though he has been advertised for and sought out all these years nothing has been heard of him. The presumption therefore is—any Court of Equity in the kingdom would presume it—that Philip Hardy is dead; and if he is dead the property goes to the heirs-at-law and legal repre- sentatives—which in this case are them as was nearest akin to him. Do you follow me ? "

" Ay, we follow you reyt enough," observed the shoemaker ; " but was not this Philip wed ? Didn't he leave no heirs, and if he did, wouldn't the property go to them ? "

" He was married—to an Italian woman I think —but his wife died and left him with a little lass, and as nothing can be heard of her neither, it is

supposed that she predeceased her father. If she
did not, we may be quite sure as she would have
come forward to claim her inheritance before now.
The same argument as I have just used applies to
her; the courts will presume as she is dead, and
you have only to prove that you are the next-of-kin
to get all this brass."

"Who has it now?"

"John Hardy's trustees. But if we establish
our claim they will have to give it to the rightful
heirs, and, to do 'em justice, I don't think they
want aught else. The estate is at present managed
by Artful and Higginbottom, highly respectable
London solicitors, I dare say, but as they make a
nice penny out of it every year, they will naturally
keep it in their hands as long as they can. They
reckon to believe, and they have persuaded the
trustees, as there is still a possibility of Philip
Hardy or his daughter turning up. But that is all
nonsense [with a knowing smile]; we know what
that means. It means as Artful and Higginbottom
don't want to lose a business as brings 'em in a
thousand or two a year. Just keep these two facts
in your mind: that there's two millions of money
in London, and that if you can prove that the John
Hardy as left it is the same John Hardy as left this
town a young man sixty-five years since it is
yours."

"Can that be proved?" asked the blacksmith.

"I have not the least doubt it can, with a little patience, and, considering the amount involved, at a very trifling cost, too. There is only one difficulty in the way—that of identifying the Calder John Hardy with the London John Hardy."

"You'll find that rayther a hard nut to crack, Mr. Ferret, I'm thinking," observed one of his listeners.

"Not at all; anyhow, not as hard as you may think. To begin with, they bore the same name and were born in the same year. That is beyond dispute. Then we know that shortly after John Hardy left Calder, a John Hardy got a situation in a London wholesale warehouse, and got on so well that it was not long before his masters took him into partnership. Then he rose to be head of the firm, and made a large fortune by speculations in land. But he never told where he came from, nor acknowledged any kinsfolk, and till he married lived in lodgings. You will happen say that is against us. But wait a minute. The John Hardy that left Calder sixty-five years since went away in a hurry. He had good reasons for not coming back or letting on where he had gone."

"What had he done?" asked one of the farmers wives.

"Well, it is a long time since," said the lawyer, "and I don't like raking up old scandals; but I could tell you, and I may have to do before we have done."

"I know what it wor, though nobody never towd me," put in the calico-weaver, with a smile and a wink. "It wor a woman. Whenever owt goes wrong you may mak sure as a woman's at bottom on it."

"Well, I believe it was something of the sort," said Ferret, when the laughter which this sally provoked had subsided. "I shall name no names, but his sweetheart played him false, and a man he looked on as a friend did him an ill turn. John was high-tempered, and he gave his treacherous friend such a beating that his life was despaired of. If he had not gone away, or if he had come back or been caught, he would have been transported as sure as a gun. So you see everything fits in, and if I could get access to John Hardy's private papers, I am sure that something might be found as would stamp him as the real Simon Pure."

"Simon Pure!" broke in the shoemaker indignantly; what's the use o' stamping him as Simon Pure? We want to stamp him as John Hardy o' Calder, and get his brass. That is what we want; isn't it, chaps?"

The audience greeted this observation with loud applause; and Ferret, to the satisfaction of everybody, explained that he had spoken in metaphor, and that Simon Pure was in no way connected with the Hardy fortune. That done, he was allowed to proceed.

" When I file my bill I shall of course demand copies of all documents bearing on the case. That will be the first step. At present the trustees deny me access to the documents. It is for you to say whether I shall act or not, and how soon. Another point : As most of you know, John Hardy was the youngest son of Nathan Hardy, who died nearly seventy years since. He left seven other sons, all of whom are deceased. All here, I think, are their children, or wives or husbands of their children. Most of them are in humble circumstances, I believe ; but a few, like our worthy chairman here, are well off. Among the poor ones are the descendants of John Hardy's eldest brother, Samuel by name, and they, according to law, would be entitled to all the real estate. But, as I have said, they are poor, and so are willing to enter into a binding arrangement to put the whole of the fortune into a common fund and divide it, share and share alike, among all Nathan Hardy's descendants. The question now before us is the raising of a sufficient sum to make good your claim. We may want two thousand pounds, but one thousand will be enough to start with. As the claimants number fifty that is not much ; only twenty pounds a-piece ; and we propose to form a limited liability concern, to be called " The Hardy Fortune Company," with two thousand shares of a pound a-piece, first issue one thousand ; and we

propose further, with the concurrence of all concerned, to pay each shareholder, on the realisation
of the fortune, a bonus of ten pounds a share. I
have so much confidence in the thing, gentlemen,
that I am prepared to take some shares myself,
unless you want to keep 'em all in the family."

"And I," said the chairman pompously, "I shall
take two hundred and fifty shares, a fourth of the
entire first issue. Now, we are not all rich, as Mr.
Ferret lately observed, but I know as there's some
of you as has got something nice laid by, and I am
sure of this, as you could not have a better invest-
ment than these 'ere shares."

"How much will it mak' a-piece?" asked the
woman with the market-basket.

"That depends on how many shares you take, Jane."

"I mean th' fortin, not th' shares."

"Well, as there's fifty of us, and th' fortune is
about two millions, that will be forty thousand
a-piece; but, to be on the safe side, say thirty
thousand."

"And how much is the shares, sayen yo'?"

"A pound a-piece."

"Well, yo' see, my mon couldn't come—he's
most terrible throng spreading muck just now—
but I'm his loeful wife, and he said as I could act
for him."

"Nobody better, I am sure, Jane," put in the
chairman gallantly.

"He said as I could act for him, and we are willing, him and me—how much did yo' say them theere shares wor?"

"Twenty shillings."

"Well, put us down for hoaf a one— and here, yo' had happen better tak' th' brass while yo're at it."

And with that she clapped down on the table four half-crowns."

All laughed, save the lawyer and the chairman, one of whom was highly indignant, the other enraged almost past speaking.

"Ten shillings for a chance of getting thirty thousand pounds!" exclaimed Ferret. "Why it is perfectly ridiculous. Besides, you cannot have half a share."

"Of course she cannot," said the chairman. "Ten shillings! Why, what are you thinking of, Jane? You have hundreds of pounds laid by; I know you have."

"Well, I will not deny as we have a bit o' summat, and we mean to keep it, my mon and me. A bird i' th' hand is worth two i' th' bush, you know. But do you really think now, Sammy, as this is a gradely good thing?"

The chairman winced. For a man of means and a justice of the peace to be called Sammy in public by Abel Hardy's wife, although she was "a bit of a relation," was an indignity which in other

circumstances he would have felt bound to resent.
But as things were, he thought it his duty to
pocket the affront and answer the question.

"Do I think it a good thing? Of course I do.
Do you suppose I should put £250 into a thing as I
didn't think well of?"

"No, to do yo' justice I don't think you would,
Sammy, nor yet 250 farthings, and yo' wi' moor
brass than yo' knowen what to do wi'. Well, mak'
it thirty shillings moor, Mr. Ferret, and if my mon's
willing we'll put wer names down for four pounds."

Encouraged by this beginning most of the
Hardys present subscribed something or another,
the total amounting, as the lawyer presently
announced, to £500.

"We shall make it up, I think," observed Mr.
Samuel Hardy.

"Not a doubt of it," answered Ferret briskly.
"There's ever so many more I have my eye on as
are good for a twenty pun note a-piece, and some
of them here as have not subscribed to-day are sure
to come forward later on. And there's many an
outsider as would be fain to have an interest in a
promising speculation like this. We could get the
money twice over, I do believe, Mr. Hardy. Yes"
(to the blacksmith), "business is over for to-day.
When there is anything further to report you will
hear from me. I am in daily communication with
Mr. Hardy on the subject, and I almost think we

should form a standing committee. We will talk about that another time. Sufficient for the day, you know. Here, Warton!" (to his clerk). "Oh, you have entered up the minutes, I see. Take these papers, will you? Mr. Hardy has been good enough to ask me to tea. Good evening, gentlemen, good evening."

As Warton left the room he was joined by Balmaine.

"What do you think of it all?" asked the clerk in a whisper. "Come down with me into the bar; the governor will not be at the office again to-night and I have something to say to you."

CHAPTER V.

THE bar of the Cock was no less quaint and old-fashioned than its club-room. It had a low, raftered ceiling, recessed windows, fitted with settles, and wainscoted walls, round which ran a broad red-cushioned oaken bench. A bright copper kettle hissed on the hob-end of a wide-throated grate of ancient make, and on the lead-lined counter was marshalled a formidable array of crystal tumblers, pewter tankards, and portly decanters, above which rose a tier of brass-bound barrels, which proclaimed in big fat letters the nature of their contents. The pervading odour of the bar was whisky and lemons, with a strong dash of tobacco; for the "Cock's" customers made it a rule never to drink ale when they could afford anything stronger.

At one end of the counter sat the landlady, Mrt. Juniper, short, broad, and rosy-cheeked. Several of the Hardy family were taking a glass to help them on their way home, and talking noisily, and generally all at once, about the late meeting, and the Hardy fortune.

" What a gabble ! " observed the lawyer's clerk
to his companion, as they stood at the bar door.
" There's no talking here, that is clear."

" I think there's a great deal of talking,"
returned his companion with a smile.

" I mean there's no chance of our having the
quiet talk I was promising myself. However, I
dare say Mrs. Juniper will let us go into her
parlour. I'll ask her."

" Good evening, Mrs. Juniper " (addressing the
landlady). " Mr. Balmaine and I have a bit of
private business to talk over, and if your parlour is
not occupied, I thought, perhaps, you would let us
sit down there a few minutes."

" Certainly, Mr. Warton ; go in and stop as long
as you like. You are quite welcome, I am sure.
Sally will take your order."

" What will you have, Balmaine ? " asked Warton,
as they stepped into the cosy little parlour behind
the bar, which Mrs. Juniper reserved for her own
particular use, and occasionally for that of a favoured
guest. " Whisky ? "

" No, I thank you ; whisky is a bad thing to work
on, and I have work to do. I think I should prefer
tea. I have some proofs to read, but they will not
be ready for an hour or more, and the paper to make
up before I go home."

" All right ; tea let it be then. Tea and toast.
And look here, Sally, give us some of the Cock's

3*

dead pig—a collop of your famous home-cured, you know. No objection to a bit of broiled ham, have you, Balmaine ? "

" None whatever. I vote for ham."

" Proposal carried *nem. con.* Tea, toast, and broiled ham as soon as you can, Sally, if you please. I am most terribly sharp set."

" Well, what is it all about, Warton ? " asked Balmaine, when they were alone. " Something I can use for the paper ? "

" Not exactly. That is always the way with you journalists. You never see, or read, or hear anything, that your first thought is not whether you cannot turn it to account for your paper. It is a good sign, though, and you will make your mark as a journalist, mark me if you don't. Here the clerk laughed as if he thought he had made an excellent joke. " But about your question. Before I answer it, let me ask you one ;—What did you think of our meeting ? "

" What does my opinion signify ? However, Ferret's theory, assuming his statements to be accurate, struck me as being rather plausible, and a fortune of two millions—can it really be so much ? —is certainly worth looking after. But do you think the Calder Hardys will be allowed to have it all to themselves ? Hardy is not a very uncommon name, and when the facts become more widely known there will be as many claimants as there are pounds."

" Exactly. And that is not all. I do not believe in the governor's theory, and I am not sure that he believes it himself."

" Not believe it himself! What does it all mean then? Why is he getting up this company? "

" I suppose because he wants to turn an honest penny."

" An honest penny! " exclaimed Balmaine indignantly.

" Perhaps I ought to have said a lawyer's honest penny. You see, we have a big office—four clerks besides myself—and Ferret has a big family—nine sons and daughters—and they cannot be kept for nothing. We are bound to have business, and prosecuting claims and filing bills help Ferret to pay his bills."

" Well, you may say what you like, Warton; but if Ferret is getting up this company, and taking these people's money to prosecute a claim he knows to be illusory, it is nothing less than a downright swindle. By Jove! I'll expose it in the paper.'

" Confound your paper! you have got it on your brain, I think. No, no; you must not do anything of the sort, Balmaine," broke in the clerk, whom his friend's threat seemed greatly to alarm; " that would be a slander, and Ferret would both prosecute you criminally and sue you for swinging damages; and I don't know, you know, that he is not sincere. It is only a case of suspicion, and I may be mistaken. Even if the chance of getting these two millions is ever so remote, it may be worth spending a thousand pounds or two to try. And really, old Ferret is not so bad, after all. Many a one would have asked for five thousand, and got it. He has formed one theory, I have formed another; that is all."

"That means, I suppose, that Ferret is not quite as big a rogue as he might be. And what is your theory, Warton?"

"I am going to tell you, and I am in a better position to judge than anybody else, for I went to London to look into the thing, and it is really on my report, though not on my opinion, that Ferret is acting. He will have it that Philip Hardy and his daughter—I forget what her outlandish name is (looking at a memorandum book)—Vera, yes, that is her name, Vera—he will have it that Philip and Vera Hardy are dead. Now, I am not at all sure of that. Where is the proof? That is what I say—where is the proof?"

"Ten years' silence and the impossibility of finding them, the absence of any news whatever about them, are as strong presumptive proofs as you could well have, I should say."

"Not in the circumstances. This Philip Hardy was one of those wild, harum-scarum fellows that never do anything like anybody else. He was a bit of a poet, and a bit of a painter—a terrible

Radical and Red Republican, and hand and glove with Mazzini and Garibaldi and that lot. He might have lived like a lord in England; his father would have bought him an estate, or done anything for him in reason, if he would only have stayed at home and settled down. But he preferred to ramble about the Continent, especially Italy, conspiring against the Austrians, and organising revolutionary societies. And, queerest thing of all, he did not care a button-top for money! When he married that Italian woman, and his father told him he would cut him off with a shilling, he just wrote back to say as he was very glad to hear it, that it would relieve him from a great responsibility. What do you think of that now? He must have been mad, don't you think?"

"Decidedly—as a March hare," returned Balmaine with a smile. "A man who refuses to be a million-aire deserves——"

"To be milled," suggested the clerk with a laugh at his own pleasantry.

"To be put in a lunatic asylum, I was going to say. But where did you learn all this, Warton?"

"From Artful and Higginbottom, and Baggs, their head clerk. They don't show any unwilling-ness to give information—not they; but I thought it might be as well to supplement it by a talk with old Baggs, so I stood him a dinner at the Bull's Head in Holborn, and it was worth while. You can talk more freely to a man across a dinner-table, when there is nothing between you and him but a bottle of port wine, than when he's sitting on an office stool with a pen behind his ear. I did not try to pump the old boy, I let the wine do that; and when he warmed to his work he told me all he knew, and as he has been in the office over forty years, and was well acquainted with both the Hardys, and all the correspondence about the estate passed through his hands, he knew a good deal."

"Does he think the father and daughter are dead?"

"Bless you, no! That's not the theory of the office at all. You see, Philip Hardy, when he went about Italy, conspiring and that, did not always go under his own name, and Artful thinks—and Baggs thinks as he thinks—as he must have been caught by the Austrians just about the time of his father's death and sentenced to a long term of imprisonment in a fortress—as likely as not for ten years—and they would not be surprised if he turned up any day. But not a word of this to anybody else. Ferret would knock my head off, and worse, if he knew."

"What could he do worse than knock your head off?" asked Balmaine, with a laugh.

"Give me the sack. If he knocked my head off, Mary and the children would get my insurance

brass—that's a thousand pounds; but if old Ferret
gave me the sack, there would be nothing for any
of us, don't you see?"

"Perfectly. All the same, I hope you will keep
your head on your shoulders. But tell me now, do
you think that Philip Hardy is really a prisoner in
some Austrian dungeon?"

"It's possible—everything is possible in this best
of possible worlds—but not, I should say, very
probable. Artful and Higginbottom think so, of
course, for reasons aforesaid, assigned by old Ferret.
They say they have made every inquiry and advertised no end. All the same, I am strongly of
opinion that if a right sharp fellow were entrusted
with the job, he would find a clue to the mystery."

"Yourself, for instance?"

"Why, yes," said the clerk. "I think I could
manage it as well as most folks. But wait a minute.
You must not think that all this talk is to lead to
nothing. I mean business, Balmaine. That girl,
you know—where is the girl? A girl with two
millions is worth finding. And she is about seventeen now and, I dare say, as handsome as paint.
Old Baggs says her father was as fine a looking
man as you would wish to see. Gad! if I was
only single! But I am not, and I cannot stir out of
Calder—got too many clogs on my feet for that.
Look here, Balmaine, you are the man that must
find Vera Hardy."

"I! What on earth do you mean, Warton?"

"I'll tell you; but you must know that I am most terribly anxious to increase my income. My Mary is a very good wife, and it isn't her fault, poor lass; but three children in less than two years is rather hard on a chap, isn't it now? If we go on at that rate I don't know whatever we shall do. It's awful to think how many of us there will be in, say, ten years. And there's as many as the pasture will keep already. If I could only find this Vera Hardy!"

"How would that help you? You could not marry her."

"I know that; but don't you think that if I let her know what an heiress she is, and helped her to her property, she would stand a handsome commission?"

"That's very likely, I think. I know I should be very happy to pay anybody who put me in the way of getting two millions a very handsome commission indeed. But what can I do in the matter?"

"You are going to take this situation in Switzerland, are you not?"

"The assistant editorship of the *Helvetic News*, you mean? Yes, I think so. The pay is no better than I am getting here, but it will be a new experience for me, and perhaps lead to something better later on."

"Quite right. You are at the top of the tree here. You can never be more than editor of the *Calder Mercury*. If you keep pegging away till you are a grey old man you will never make more than three or four pounds a week, and yet you have it in you to be a slap-up journalist. Well, when you go to Switzerland, I want you to find Miss Hardy."

"You are joking, Warton. What chance shall I have of finding the poor girl?'

"A good many, I hope. Philip Hardy was sometimes in Switzerland—that we do know—and when not there he was in Italy, and they are about as close together as Lancashire and Yorkshire, they tell me. You are sure to be going about, and when you do you must just ask questions and keep your eyes open. I will post you up before you set off, and—who knows? you will maybe light on her. And if you do we will go snacks at the commission. Suppose she stands five per cent., why that would be a hundred thousand pounds! Fifty thousand a-piece! I would not object to a baby a twelve-month then, and they might keep on coming for a quarter of a century, bless 'em, if they liked! What do you say?"

"About the babies?"

"No, about finding this girl."

"I fear the chance of my finding her is very remote; but I will keep the matter in mind, and do my best. I don't think, though, I should like to ask her for a commission."

" Why ? Isn't it business ? "

" Perhaps. I was not thinking of that. But I could not fancy myself going to a young girl saying, ' You are heiress to a fine fortune, promise me a commission of five per cent. and I will give you all particulars.' "

" But you might tell her first and claim the commission afterwards."

" I could not do even that, Warton."

The clerk's countenance fell.

" Why ? What is there wrong in it ? A ship captain who takes a derelict vessel into port gets salvage, and the finder of a purse is rewarded by the owner."

" Do you think I would take a reward for finding a purse ? " asked Balmaine indignantly.

" Perhaps not ; but I'll take all the money I can get hold of as is honestly come by. However, if you won't ask her yourself, you will perhaps not object to my asking her, on the ground that I am a professional man, and put you up—gave the information that enabled you to find her."

" None whatever ; that would be entirely your own affair. But this is very absurd, you know. I shall never find the girl. Remember, it is ten years since all this happened."

"At any rate you can try, if only for the poor girl's sake. Who knows where she is?"

"Precisely; who knows where she is?"

"That we must try to find out. After all, the world is very small. How often we run against people we least expect to meet! Why, when I was in London the other day I ran into the arms— literally ran into the arms—of my old schoolfellow, Harry Welsh. He went to America seven years since, and had landed only three days before! What do you think of that now!"

"But, you see, the misfortune is," laughed Balmaine, "that if Miss Hardy were to run into my arms I should not know her."

"I wish she would run into your arms; you would soon identify her, I'll be bound, and—what a happy thought!—perhaps marry her. Then you would be paid for your trouble, and no mistake, and could afford me a swinging commission."

"Rubbish! May I beg of you not to talk such nonsense, Warton. I have not the least hope of finding this girl, and I am sure I shall not marry her."

"Perhaps you are bespoke," replied the clerk, eyeing keenly his companion, who had spoken somewhat warmly, and seemed rather taken aback. "And that reminds me. I have heard a bit of a whisper, but I did not believe there was aught in it. I would not if I were you, Balmaine. I——"

"Here is the tea," interrupted Balmaine coldly. "Put the tray opposite Mr. Warton, Sally, and the ham at this end of the table."

"How confoundedly touchy he is!" thought the clerk. "But it looks like being a true bill, and if it is I shall be sorry. Balmaine should do better in every way than marry Lizzie Hardy. I don't like the lot, and if I see any chance of stopping it, by Jingo, I will."

"Take some ham, Warton?" asked Balmaine when Sally had taken her departure.

"Thank you, I will take some ham. A 'cute old boy is Saintly Sam. Don't you think it's right I am?"

"Why, what put him into your head?" said Balmaine with a rather forced laugh.

"Ham—don't you perceive that it rhymes with Sam?"

"You should not speak evil of dignities, Warton. Mr. Hardy has been three times mayor of Calder, remember, and is at this present moment a justice of the peace, and otherwise a man of importance in the borough."

"Exactly; and does not that make his conduct on the present occasion all the meaner?"

"In what way?"

"In what way! Why, don't you see that he doesn't more than half believe in this Hardy fortune, and yet he is persuading his poor kinsfolk to lay out £750 in trying to get it! You will say, perhaps, that he goes in for £250 on his own hook. But what is that for a man like him, when there is a chance of getting forty thousand? Wouldn't it have looked a fine sight better, think you, if he had spent a couple of hundreds or so in preliminary inquiries before sending the hat round?—for that's what it amounts to. And I am by no means sure that he means to find the two-fifty after all."

"You surely don't mean to say, Warton, that he will attempt to back out of a promise so publicly made?"

"Not he! Saintly Sam knows a trick worth two of that! He'll take the shares, right enough; but, unless I am mistaken, he has an understanding with old Ferret to allow him a commission of five or ten per cent. on the amount subscribed, or to do his own business on special terms for so long."

"Come, come, Warton, you let your dislike of the man carry you too far. Hardy has his faults, I admit, but he is not a miser."

"I never said he was. A miser does not spend money on himself. Hardy does; he likes to live well, and be a big pot. To hear him talk you would think he was generosity itself; but just you try him! Anybody that has aught to do with Saintly Sam is pretty sure to get hold of the dirty end of the stick. However, as he's a friend of yours I won't say aught against him."

"Not say aught against him! I don't know what you could well say more! Anyhow, he has always behaved well to me."

"Of course he has. You are the editor of the *Mercury*, and have been useful to him, and may be again; but just you try the other tack and you'll see. But let us drop the old beggar and talk about something else. You will not be setting out for Switzerland just yet, I suppose?"

"Oh dear no; I only sent in my acceptance to-day, and until it is acknowledged, and the appointment confirmed, I cannot very well give Grindleton notice, you know; and that reminds me (looking at his watch), it is quite time I went to the office and made up the paper."

"Well, we must have another talk or two about this Hardy business before you set sail. The subject is far from being exhausted."

"Whenever you like. But as to my obtaining any information about Philip Hardy, or finding his daughter, I really don't think there is a vestige of hope."

"Hope be hanged!" returned the clerk, thumping a fat fist on the table. "I have made up my mind to bottom this business, and bottom it I will —if you will help me."

"Of course I will. Have I not said so?"

"Energetically?"

"Energetically."

"It's a bargain, then," exclaimed the clerk, slapping his hand into that of his friend. "And look here; I'll put it all down on paper—write you out a brief, in fact, embodying the latest information on the subject. I don't mean to let the thing slip out of your mind, I can tell you."

Then, after an amicable contest as to who should pay, which resulted in favour of the clerk, they went into the bar and settled with Mrs. Juniper.

CHAPTER VI.

THE Hardys had gone, and the "Cock's" regular company of gossips and topers were dropping in and settling down to their usual drinking bout in the bar.

In an arm-chair by the fireside sat Humphrey Hutton, one of Calder's most remarkable citizens, a big, stout, florid man, with great red whiskers and a ruddy countenance. Every evening of his life Humphrey (who was a miller by trade and looked well after his business), when he had taken his tea and had washed and dressed himself, walked up to the "Cock," took his accustomed place near the hearth, and stayed there until he had drunk his "allowance." And as he seemed none the worse for his libations, and looked the very picture of health, people naturally thought his potations did him more good than harm; and as he died at last by falling into his own mill-dam when he was perfectly sober, nobody could say that whisky had shortened his days, or that, if he had not swallowed more water than agreed with him, he might not have lived as long as anybody else.

Another faithful frequenter of the " Cock's " bar was Bob Rogers, plasterer and house-painter. His jovial face beamed with good-humour; he sang a good song, told a good story, and, though he liked a glass, never got drunk, which was more than could be said of his wife. Once upon a time, after she had been indulging overmuch, she ran away, fearing her husband's wrath. When she returned, Bob took a stick to her. " I am not licking thee for running away," he exclaimed between each thwack; " I am licking thee for coming back ageean."

Bob's inseparable companion was Kit Brown, master blacksmith, a man of means and a church-warden—though if you had seen him shoeing a horse, and heard him damning a hostler, you would not have thought so. He made a capital foil to his friend Rogers. A giant in bulk, Kit had a saturnine face and an aquiline nose, could no more make a joke or sing a song than his own bellows, was shy in company, and rarely ventured beyond an occasional " Well, I'll be d——d " when anything particularly pleased or surprised him. But he could drink even more than the miller; and though from motives of economy he did not often take above half-a-dozen glasses at a sitting, he had been known to " knock off " a score without any other visible effect than making him a little more silent than usual.

4*

"Why, here's Mr. Balmaine and Mr. Warton," exclaimed Rogers. "Good-day to you. Willn't you sit down and have summat?"

"Thank you," said Balmaine; "I have work to do. I cannot stay. Good-night, Warton."

"Well, yo'll take a sup o' summat with us, Mr. Warton?"

The clerk, thinking of Mary and the children, hesitated, shook his head, and made as if he, too, was going away.

"Sit down, man, sit down; yo're not i' that horry, I know. Make him sit down, Kit."

The blacksmith laid his huge hand on Warton's shoulder, whereupon the clerk, although he was a stout little fellow enough, dropped on the oaken bench as if he had been shot.

"I'll stan'," said Kit.

"That is because you have made me sit, I suppose," laughed Warton, who never lost a chance of making a joke.

"What mon it be?" asked Kit solemnly. He never took a joke in, however palpable, under five minutes.

"If I must put myself outside something, let it be whisky."

"A whisky for Mr. Warton," shouted the smith, and then relapsed into reflective silence.

"Young Balmaine seems throng just now," observed Flip, the auctioneer, a little old fellow

with a cracked voice and an inflamed face, who once
in his life, and once only, had put on a pair of
trousers, but not being able to abide " them things
dangling about his legs," he speedily doffed them and
resumed the breeches of his forefathers. Flip, it
need hardly be said, was as conservative in the
domain of politics as in the matter of costume, and
never went to the " Cock " without expressing the
opinion that the country was going to " rack and
ruin along o' these 'ere Radicals."

" Yes," said Warton, " he finds plenty to do, for
when he is not editing the *Mercury*, he is writing
for other papers—not always in them, though, I am
afraid."

" A terrible downcoming for that family," put in
Ward, the vet.—an observation which he had
probably made five hundred times before in the very
same place.

"It is that," said Bob Rogers sympathetically,
" and I feel right sorry for 'em. How nobody suspected owt o' th' sort, afore old Mr. Balmaine
died, caps me. We could all see it plain enough
after."

" Ay, after-wit is a complaint as most Englishmen
is troubled with at times. And how well them lads
faced it."

" They did that, and a most terrible knockdown
blow it was, too. So did Miss Balmaine."

" Ay, she' a rare fine lass, and gradely good to th'

owd woman, they tell me. Has owt been heard of
Bradley yet ? "

" No ; and he'll tak good care as there isn't.   He
was not called Billy Godeeper for nowt.   What a
scoundrel that chap turned out to be sure !   Mony's
th' time as he has sat i' that theer cheer fratching
(boasting) how well he was doing, and what good
investments he was making for Mr. Balmaine and
a twothry more on 'em !   It is my firm opinion
as ——"

" Well, I'll be d——d ! "

And as the blacksmith uttered this not very
original, or, on the face of it, particularly funny
speech, he indulged in a peal of Homeric laughter
that shook the glasses on the table, and so startled
Sally that she dropped her tray, and half-a-dozen
whisky tumblers and a jug of hot water went crash
on the floor.

" Why, whatever's to do, thou great crazy beggar ?
What is there to laugh at ? " exclaimed Bob Rogers,
looking angrily at his friend.

" I wor nobut thinking," answered Kit, struggling
with his mirth ; "I wor nobbut thinking o' what
Mr. Warton said just now, when I said as I'd stan'.
Gradely good, worn't it ?   Sup up, Mr. Warton, and
I'll stan' another.   It is woth two glasses, that is.
Sup up ! "

And the smith, thinking, probably, that example
was better than precept, suited the action to the

word; but resuming his laugh rather too soon, the
consequences were disastrous in the extreme, and
Kit narrowly escaped being choked.

While the company at the " Cock " were discuss-
ing his family and their affairs, Balmaine was walking rapidly down a steep street towards the office of
the *Mercury*. " Calder," as a local rhymester wrote,
" crowns a rocky height," and, in truth, there is not
a level street in it. The town, which clusters round
the lofty ruins of a mediæval castle, though it
figured in the Wars of the Roses and the Great
Rebellion—has a history which dates back to the
times of Alfred and Cnut, and has returned great
statesmen to Parliament, is looked upon by its more
enterprising neighbours as effete and played out.
It has no coal-fields, is a long way from seaports
and markets, and albeit there are three or four
cotton factories and bobbin mills, turned by water
power, which seem to do pretty well, the new men
don't take to Calder, and the population, which was
never great, rather diminishes than increases. But
it lies on the borders of two counties, in the midst
of a rich agricultural district; its corn and cattle
and hay markets are important and largely fre-
quented, and its weekly newspaper, though the circulation was not very extensive, had sufficient
advertisements to make it a profitable enterprise.

The editorial offices were in a side street off the
main thoroughfare, and to reach them Balmaine

had to go up a dark entry and mount a flight of
wooden stairs. The room into which he entered
and where he did most of his work, was as gaunt
and bare as an anchorite's cave or a monk's cell. The
walls were unpapered, and the floor was black with
the ink-slingings of a century of editors—for the
Mercury had lived a hundred years. A big, square
table, littered with copy and proofs, a few chairs and
a book-case, made up the furniture. The table was
lighted, but not the room, by a couple of gas-
burners under green shades, and on one of the
chairs sat a small boy, with an extremely dirty face,
and wide-open mouth, fast asleep.

"Hallo, Jeremiah!" shouted Balmaine, at the
same time throwing a folded paper, with aim
so accurate, that it dropped into the lad's
mouth like a ball into a socket, making him
look as if he were developing news from his inner
consciousness.

"Yes, sir," said Jeremiah, opening his eyes and
spitting out the newspaper.

" Is anything wanted ? "

" Yes; they want them proofs; and · Methuselah
has been here—he waited ever so long, and said as
if you wanted him, he'd be round at the 'Lord
Nelson.' "

" Go to the 'Lord Nelson' and ask him to come
here, and then run down to the post-office for the
letters."

Then he sat down to his proofs. A few minutes afterwards the door opened.

" Is that you, Methuselah ? "

" I believe it is."

He was not a very old man, not more than fifty probably, but when he came to Calder, a dozen years previously, as reporter for the *Mercury,* he persistently refused to disclose ¡his age—a point as to which the Calderites were very curious. To punish his obstinacy they called him Methuselah—a name which in the end so completely superseded his own that he was hardly known by any other.

" Have you extended your notes of last night's ratepayers' meeting ? " asked Balmaine.

" Certainly. Here are the proofs," said the reporter, who had brought into the room a powerful odour of tobacco. He was a tall, angular man, with lantern jaws, a purple nose, and a snuffy voice. " Would you like to cast your eye over them ? "

" Do they contain anything libellous ? Speakers at ratepayers' meetings don't always use the most measured language."

" Well, nothing exactly libellous was said, but something not very pleasant was."

" About whom ? "

" About us."

" What was it ? "

" Somebody quoted the *Mercury* and mentioned Mr Grindleton and you, and Horseball—the Radical toffee-dealer, you know—and said if there was a bigger fool in Calder than the editor of the *Mercury* it was the proprietor."

" Not complimentary, certainly, but hardly actionable," said Balmaine laughing. " Have you got it in your report ? "

" Yes ; but I will strike it out if you like."

" No ; let it stand. Editors should not be thin-skinned ; we must give and take, you know. Ah ! here comes the letters."

There was quite a bundle of them. Some were thrown into the waste-paper basket as fast as they were read, others were placed under a weight on the table, and one, the perusal of which seemed to give Balmaine considerable satisfaction, and contained a slip of printed matter, found its way into his pocket.

Then followed two hours' hard work and a visit to the printing-office, and shortly before eleven o'clock the editor wended his way homeward.

CHAPTER VII.

CORA.

THE night was fine ; a bright moon shone in a clear sky, and a brisk walk of twenty minutes, on a limestone road shaded by trees, brought Balmaine to a bridge that spanned a broad and babbling brook. Here he turned down a lane running between tall hedgerows until he came to a little white gate. This he opened, and the next moment was at the door of an ivy-mantled cottage with a wooden porch over which grew a climbing rose-tree. There was an odour of southernwood and mignonette, a scent of new-mown hay ; the pebbled music of the brook, as it coursed through the meadows below, was borne faintly on the dying breeze ; and, bathed in the golden moonlight, the cottage, with its fruit-trees and roses and cascades of ivy falling over quaint dormer windows, looked like a little paradise whose inmates must needs be free from sordid wants and corroding care—the abode of peace, contentment, and love.

Before Balmaine set his foot on the threshold the door opened.

" I knew your step," said a low, sweet voice. " I
have been expecting you nearly an hour. Are you
not rather later than usual on a Friday night ? "

" Yes ; I went to the Hardy meeting, and had a
long talk with Warton, and I had more proofs to
read than I expected."

" You must be hungry, then. Come in and have
your supper."

The room into which Balmaine entered, though
small, low ceiled, and simply furnished, bore
evidence in all its arrangements of refined tastes
and gentle culture. The white window curtains
were gracefully disposed, colours harmonized ; in
the middle of the table, which was laid for supper,
stood a vase of flowers, and opposite to it were a
little jardinière and an open cottage pianoforte,
whereon lay a book of Mendelssohn's music. There
was also a small bookcase, and the walls were
adorned with several water-colour sketches—of no
great merit, perhaps, but pleasant to look upon for
all that.

Between the young girl and him whom she so
graciously welcomed there was so much likeness as
to leave little doubt that they were nearly akin.
Cora Balmaine, though of attractive appearance,
had a head and face rather too small for her height ;
yet the head was shapely and the face comely—the
hair dark brown ; long lashes shaded eyes of bright
hazel, which, together with her slightly aquiline

nose, square jaws, full red lips, and broad white
brow, suggested a character at once tender and
strong, and a sweet and womanly temper. Her
kinsman, albeit his features bore a general and
unmistakable resemblance to hers, was far from
being cast in precisely the same mould. Being
much larger, there was not the same disproportion
between the frame and the head; the nose was,
perhaps, more aquiline; the jaws, though their
contour was somewhat disguised by a short curly
beard, seemed squarer; the hair was slightly darker,
and while her complexion was high his was almost
colourless; but the eyes were of the same shade,
and the face of one, as well as of the other, wore
an expression of gravity, almost of sadness, that
hardly befitted their years, for neither could be much
more than twenty-three or four.

" How has mother been ? " was the young man's
first question.

" As usual, very low, and sometimes suffering;
but she seems a little better this afternoon, and
Dr. Foster thought he could see a slight gleam of
improvement."

" Poor mother! I wish she could be herself
again. What a relief it would be for us all—for
you especially, Cora ! It is very hard on you, and
even yet I do not feel quite satisfied that I have
acted rightly in taking this situation. It looks like
deserting one's post."

" But you have written to accept it, Alfred ? "

" Yes; as we agreed yesterday. I was bound to write to-day, but I wrote very reluctantly."

" The reluctance is natural, and I shall be very sorry to lose you, but I have not a doubt that you are right. You may never have such another chance, and it would be one of those blunders that are worse than a crime to let it slip. Here at Calder you are simply wasting your time, and I want you, Alfred—I want you to be somebody, as I am sure you will if you have a fair chance. We have a stimulus others do not possess; they are merely struggling to rise, we are struggling to rise again—to retrieve a lost position."

" What pluck you have, Cora ! " was Alfred's admiring comment on the lady's little speech.

" So have you. I would not give a fig for a spiritless man."

" Well, whatever other faults I may have, I do not think I am without pluck. But you and George beat me in that respect, though."

" Dear George ! Yes, he is a dear, good, noble boy. I wrote to him to-day such a long letter."

" Talking of letters, here is something that will please you, I think."

" What is it about ? "

" That story I sent for you to the *Piccadilly Magazine*."

"And have they—have they accepted it?" demanded Cora eagerly.

"They have. See, here is the proof."

"My first proof!" exclaimed the girl, unfolding the slip with trembling fingers. "My first proof! Yes, here it is—'The Broken Tryst,' by Cora Balmaine. I never saw my name in print before, never. Oh, Freddy, I am so glad!" And Cora, who a moment before had looked so grave, broke into a ringing laugh, and clapped her hands, as she had used to do in her girlhood when anybody gave her a new toy. "But," pouting, "here are some dreadful mistakes. I am sure I never wrote this— nor this. And, if I know myself, I can, at least, spell."

"And dear me, how short it is! Surely my twenty pages of manuscript cannot be compressed into these six pages of print!"

"Very easily, I should say. It is astonishing to what an extent you can boil down copy by putting it into type. Few of those who 'glance over' an article or a story think that what they devour in five minutes, and forget in three, may have taken somebody as many hours to write."

"I hope nobody will devour my story in five minutes, and forget it in three; that would be too bad," said Cora warmly. "Why, I spent days on it, and wrote it out at least three times."

"That's always the case with young writers," replied Alfred sententiously. "They give themselves an infinity of trouble, often to little purpose. But you will become wiser with experience; '*pas trop de zèle*,' it does not pay."

"How you talk! You might be an author of experience, yet you have never written anything but newspaper articles and reviews of second-class books."

"At any rate newspaper articles deal with facts; and as for second-class books—well, that is a matter of opinion. But don't you see, you foolish girl, that I was only teasing you? You do well to take pains; but I am afraid that it will hardly pay—from a pecuniary point of view—to write a story for —shall I say a second-class magazine?—three times over."

"I was not thinking of that; and do you know, Freddy, I could not help doing my best, even if I were to get nothing for it. But, perhaps, as I acquire more skill I may be able to write more rapidly. How much do you think they will give me for this?"

"Three guineas, perhaps. I do not think the *Piccadilly* is precisely the most liberal of magazines."

"Three guineas! But that would really be very nice, you know. If I could only earn that much every month! We should be positively rich, Alfred; I could do all sorts of things. We might keep a little pony carriage to drive your mother about in, or go to the seaside, or engage another maid, and then I should have more time for writing and that; and, yes, I would have a new carpet for the drawing-room, and a new coal-scuttle."

"Castles in the air, Cora—castles in the air," said Alfred mock-seriously. "Don't indulge in extravagant dreams about fresh carpets and new coal-scuttles. You will only be disappointed; and all moralists agree that it is a very pernicious habit."

"I don't care one bit for the moralists. I must and shall build castles in the air. It is one of the few pleasures I have; and I am quite sure of this, that nobody can write stories who does not build castles in the air. And that reminds me. You have not told me anything about the meeting. Is the Hardy fortune a castle in the air or a fact?"

"A fact."

"The Hardys will get it, then?"

"Some Hardys may; but I am not sure that these Hardys will."

And then Alfred told Cora all that had passed at the meeting, and been imparted to him by the lawyer's clerk.

"It is a strange story," said Cora musingly; "but truth is often stranger than fiction, and many things happen in real life which, if they were put into novels, people would say were too extravagant to be true. You will do as Warton suggests, won't you, and try to find this girl?"

"I certainly mean to do so, as far as my limited opportunities will allow. When Warton first mooted the idea to me it seemed as if nothing could be more absurd; but the more I think of it the more it takes hold of me. Yes, I should like to ascertain Philip Hardy's fate, and find out whether the child is dead or alive."

"Poor girl! Supposing her father is in an Austrian dungeon, where can she be? Could not somebody apply to the Austrian government for information?"

"I have thought of that already; but the difficulty is that he went under several names—in order to deceive the police, I suppose—and even if the Austrians said they had no such prisoner as Philip Hardy, it would not follow that he was not in one of their dungeons. What I mean to do is this. Warton will give me a written account of all the circumstances so far as he knows them, and as I pass through London I shall call at Artful and Higginbottom's office and make a few inquiries on my own account. Then, when I get to Geneva I shall take the advice of somebody experienced in such matters as to how I ought to proceed."

"The police?"

"No; that would cost money, and I have none to spare. Some non-official person, I mean—when I can find one. But that will necessarily be after I have been there a while and got to know a few people."

" How soon do you think you shall go ? "

" That I cannot tell, until I receive my answer."

" Have you said anything to Mr. Grindleton ? "

" Not yet. I must not give up one situation before I am sure of the other."

" Cautious Alfred ! You are learning wisdom in the school of experience. Does Lizzie know that you contemplate leaving Calder ? "

This was said not unkindly, but there was a pointedness in Cora's manner, a slight touch of sarcasm in her voice, that called the colour to the young man's cheeks, and he answered rather abruptly, " Not yet; I suppose I must, though." He had evidently been hit in a weak place.

" Yes; I think she has a right to expect that attention from you. But I hope she will not find it difficult to console herself—after you are gone."

The words were hardly out of Cora's mouth when she regretted having uttered them, for this time Alfred looked really annoyed, and she felt that the fact of his having acted unwisely conferred on her no right to give him pain, was, indeed, rather a reason why she should not give him pain.

" Forgive me, Alfred," she said, speaking soft and low, as she put her arm round his neck and looked her most bewitching look, " for being so unkind. I am so sorry ; but——"

5*

"I am sorry, too, and vexed—with myself, not you. Yes, I have been a goose, and you are quite justified in telling me so."

"I did not tell you so."

"You meant it, and you think it. But never mind; let us say no more about it. Go to bed; it is quite time, and" (smiling) "dream about your new story. I suppose you will put that proof under your pillow?"

"Of course I shall. And in the morning you shall give me a lesson in proof-reading."

CHAPTER VIII.

THE BALMAINES.

ALTHOUGH they bore the same surname and were so intimate, Alfred and Cora Balmaine were not brother and sister. His father, her uncle, had been Rector of Calder. The living was one of the best in the county, and as Mr. Balmaine possessed private means and his wife a small fortune, they were in easy circumstances, spent freely, and kept up the style of a county family of the lesser sort. Their two sons, George and Alfred, between whom there was hardly a year's difference in age, were sent to a public school much affected by the aristocracy, and had each a pony, which, when they grew older, were exchanged for a couple of hunters. George was destined for the army, Alfred for the bar, and in due time the one went to Sandhurst, the other to Oxford. A few years before this came to pass their uncle Hugh, an officer in the army, died, leaving his little motherless girl alone in the world, and the Rector his sole executor. Mr. Balmaine, who had loved his brother dearly, took Cora to his own house, with the full concurrence of his wife. She was treated in every respect as their own child, and found these foster-parents as fond and devoted as her own had been. As the young people grew older it came to be understood that in the fulness of time George and Cora should make a match of it, and, contrary to the general rule in such cases, the parties chiefly concerned cordially fell in with the wishes of their elders. Childish affection ripened into ardent love, and while still in their teens they were formally engaged. There were none of the usual motives for delay. When his son should come of age and get his lieutenant's commission, the Rector proposed to assign him an allowance, which, together with the income arising from Cora's fortune, would make them a good income. The arrangement pleased everybody, and the Balmaines were one of the happiest, and, to all seeming, one of the most prosperous families in the country-side. They had only one trouble, and that was fast passing away. Alfred had not been many weeks at Oxford when he was badly hurt in a scrimmage at football. The doctors feared at first that his back was permanently injured, and that he would be a cripple for life. But with careful nursing and long resting—for more than a twelve-month he could not rise from his couch—he grew gradually better, and by the time George received his lieutenant's commission Alfred was almost as strong as ever. In one respect his illness, which lasted several years, had been to his advantage. He read and studied more than he would have done at the university, and learnt several modern

languages which were afterwards of great
use to him. He also sent several contributions,
both in prose and verse, to the *Calder Mercury,*
and his effusions were always welcomed by the
editor and admired by his readers. It thus came
to pass that Alfred Balmaine, though possessing
more book-learning than most young men of his
years, was also more unsophisticated. His life had
been passed nearly altogether at home and at
school, and his experience of the world was confined
to Calder and the neighbourhood. His father, who
was easy-tempered and good-natured to a fault,
treated him, in consideration of his illness, with
unusual indulgence ; yet in some things the Rector
was as firm as a rock. He would on no account
tolerate falsehood or meanness; his ideals were
high almost to Quixotism ; he always impressed on
his sons that a clear conscience was far above either
wealth or position ; that it was better to endure
calamity than suffer dishonour, and that a true
gentleman should be " sans peur et sans tache,"
principles to which he himself so steadfastly
adhered, and gave so wide an application, that some
people considered him a nincompoop. It was a
common saying in Calder that, though unexceptionable
as a parson, Balmaine was a fool in business,
and often allowed himself to be egregiously taken
in, for he invariably treated a man as honest until he
was shown to be a rogue—an interpretation of the

golden rule that did not always turn to his advantage, nor, as the result proved, to that of his family.

The day had been fixed for George and Cora's marriage, and preparations for the happy event were in active progress, when one evening the Rector came home from visiting a sick patient, looking ill and flushed, and complaining of headache. The next morning he was worse, and the doctor pronounced it to be a case of typhoid fever. When typhoid fever attacks elderly people, it often proves fatal, and a week later Mr. Balmaine slept his last sleep under a cypress-tree in his own churchyard.

Before the bereaved family had time to realise the full extent of their loss, another blow, hardly less crushing, fell upon them.

CHAPTER IX

MORE TROUBLES.

IF sympathy is often expressed without being felt, curiosity, on the other hand, is often felt without being expressed. The friend who condoles with you on the death of a near kinsman of reputed wealth, may or may not be sincere in his assurance of sympathy, but of a surety, he is burning to know how much the deceased has left, and for how much you figure in his last will and testament. And so at Calder, after people who met casually in the street or elsewhere, had told each other what a bad job the Rector's death was, and how greatly he had been respected, one would observe in a tone of indifference :

" You have not heard how much, I suppose ? "

" Not exactly. About fifty, I fancy. Some folks say as he had a deal of money out at interest; but Bradley is very close."

When the Rector had been laid in the ground, there was less reticence, and on the evening after the funeral, the question of what he had died worth was keenly discussed in the " Cock " bar. The estimates varied from forty to sixty thousand, and when Horseball, the Radical toffee dealer, who had no great love for " church parsons," suggested thirty, he was laughed to scorn.

" Where's Bradley ? " asked Bob Rogers, " he'd know to a penny. He knows how much everybody's worth i' this town."

But Bradley was not there—never, in fact, entered the " Cock" again. The next day it began to be rumoured that he had not been seen for three days, and was nowhere to be found, and that the Rector's executors could make neither head nor tail of his affairs. Bradley, the land agent, had been his man of business, looked after his glebe, kept his accounts, and invested his money. Then the people who were always wiser than anybody else—after the event—hinted that they had suspected all along that the land agent was no good, and should not be surprised if he had run away. And so he had; and when the fact became generally known, great was the consternation in Calder, for many of the townsfolk had intrusted him with money, and all who had trusted him were betrayed. Some were ruined outright. Among these was the Rector, albeit he had died in the full assurance that his family were amply provided for. His trust in the defaulting land agent had been boundless. He held him to be not only an honest man, but a financial genius of the first order. And financial

genius of a certain sort Bradley had indeed shown
himself. He had deceived shrewder and less trustful
men than Mr. Balmaine, and so contrived matters,
that until the Rector's death and his own flight, nobody suspected that he had been paying interest out
of his clients' capital, and that the local companies in
which he had persuaded the Rector to take so many
shares were bogus concerns of his own creation.
When the promoter disappeared, the companies
collapsed, and the liabilities arising out of them
swallowed up all the assets which Bradley had not
previously reduced to possession. Cora's fortune,
which the Rector had allowed Bradley to invest for
him, was engulphed in the general ruin, and she,
like her cousins, was left literally penniless. It was
only by the forbearance of the creditors, that Mrs.
Balmaine was allowed to receive the value of a life
assurance on her husband's life; and a few of his
parishioners bought for her, out of her own furniture,
enough to furnish a small cottage in the outskirts
of the town. George sold his commission, which
had been paid for only a few weeks before his
father's death, and the proceeds of the sale, added
to the value of the policy, made about £2,000,
which was sunk in an annuity for his mother's
benefit. Then the young fellow, who would neither
abandon the career of arms, nor be beholden to
friends, took counsel with his sweetheart, and with
her full concurrence, enlisted in a regiment under

orders for India. Cora, indeed, showed rare courage and resource; but Mrs. Balmaine, whose married life had been almost free from care, who had never known what it was to want money or have a reasonable wish ungratified, was utterly crushed. Her health suffered, her temper became querulous and exacting, and she thought herself the most unfortunate woman in the world. Cora, although her own sorrow was heavy and hard to bear, tended her aunt with untiring care and devotion, and did much to keep up the courage of the brothers.

"It is very bad," she would say. "There is no question about that. But I have read somewhere that the best way to meet trouble is to look it in the face; and there is really no cause for despair. We three are young and strong, and if we help ourselves God will help us. We can at least earn our own living, and though poor mother cannot have all the luxuries she has been used to, she can live decently and without troubling anybody. And think how much worse it might have been. Suppose this had happened when we were all children, or there had not been enough to pay your father's debts!"

Yet the parting with George tried her courage to the uttermost. Nobody—not even he—knew how much she suffered. He was going to a country where war was always possible and danger ever present, and she knew that before they could

meet again she must endure long years of appre-
hension and suspense. But Heaven had blessed her
with a brave heart and a sanguine temperament;
she had been bred in the belief that an Infinite
wisdom orders everything for the best, and though
her heart was torn her spirit never faltered.

"You are going away," she said, smiling through
her tears, "and it may be long before we meet
again. But we are both young and can wait and
hope. And you will get your commission, I know
you will, and come back a captain at least, and it
will be ever so much more creditable to rise by
merit than be promoted by purchase."

The evening before he left to join his regiment at
Portsmouth, though a sore trial, was not without a
certain melancholy satisfaction. The brothers
seemed to be more drawn to each other than they
had ever been before, to see further into each
other's hearts than they had ever yet seen, and to
love one another with a deeper love than they had
yet known.

Before they separated for the night, Cora opened
the piano and played, and they all sang, the
brothers with an arm round each other's neck,
"Lord, abide with me." Their voices were half-
choked with tears, and the same thought was in the
minds of all, "When and where shall we three meet
again?" But the beautiful hymned prayer, so full
of trust and devout feeling, brought comfort to

their souls, and they did not sorrow as those without hope. In the years to come, though they brought new trials and vicissitudes, the memory of that last evening at Heathbeck Cottage never faded from the minds of the brothers and their cousin. It marked a turning point in their destinies.

CHAPTER X.

ALFRED had of course abandoned all hope of returning to Oxford, and if it had not been for his mother
and Cora, he would have followed George's example
and accompanied him to India. He had not
acquired a profession, and knew that he had no
aptitude for business. But it was necessary for him
to do something, and he gladly accepted the editorship of the *Calder Mercury*, for which he was indebted to Warton, who had been concerned in the
winding up of his father's affairs, and was on friendly
terms with Grindleton, the proprietor of the paper.
The post was not a very lucrative one, the pay being
only three pounds a week, but the duties were
neither heavy nor uncongenial, and three pounds
a week, added to his mother's income, made £290
a year.

Cora declared that they were positively rich, and
as the emoluments of a private soldier are not
exactly princely, it was resolved to spare George £20
a year. But this George positively refused; he
would take only a pound a month so long as the
regiment was in England; his pay and allowances

in India, he said, would amply suffice for all his wants there.

For a while all went smoothly, and though the trials they had undergone made them look older and graver than quite beseemed their years, the young people were not unhappy. True, Mrs. Balmaine's health was always a source of anxiety, but the anxiety was not of that acute or agonising sort that renders life almost or altogether a burden. Then their income, though small, was sufficient, and George was able to give a good account of himself. Before leaving Portsmouth he had become a corporal, and a few months after the regiment landed in India, he got the much-coveted stripes.

" If we could only have a war," he wrote home, " I should get a commission in no time."

Cora was naturally greatly delighted, and Alfred's mind began to be much exercised as to how he, too, might better himself. Grindleton was not likely to raise his salary, and even if he were, he could not remain editor of the *Calder Mercury* to the end of his days. He had offered several contributions to the London papers, and some had been accepted, but on the whole he had not been very fortunate, for Calder, as may be supposed, was fertile neither in incidents nor topics. The idea of trying to obtain a situation in London had occurred to him, but the *Mercury's* London correspondent, whom he consulted on the subject, told him that com-

petition for employment was so keen among pressmen on the spot that his chances of success
would be extremely remote. One paper alone
that he mentioned had the names of more than
a thousand applicants on its books. It was from
the same correspondent that he heard of the
situation in Switzerland. The pay offered was
poor—no more than he was getting in Calder—
but there was a possibility of advancement, and a
certainty of enlarging his experience, both of
journalism and of life. On these grounds his friends
advised him to accept the appointment, and on this
advice, as we have seen, Balmaine resolved to act.

A few months before this came to pass, he had
enlarged his experience in a way which was now
causing him an infinity of embarrassment, and his
cousin no little annoyance. The original, if indi-
rect, cause of the trouble was a change of creed on
the part of the gentleman whom Warton had ir-
reverently denominated " Saintly Sam," and stigma-
tised as a rogue. Mr. Hardy was the owner of the
biggest factory in the borough of Calder, part proprietor of a print works, and principal proprietor in
a brewery. He liked to boast that he was a self-
made man, and was fond of pointing a moral with
the tale of his own rise in life, which he ascribed to
perseverance and integrity, and, above all, to a
strict observance of the Sabbath. Some of his
neighbours thought otherwise. They said he owed

his prosperity chiefly to cunning and cupidity. Be that as it may, he was a shining light in a small sect of Dissenters; and ran a Sunday-school in connection with his cotton factory. It was attended by the children of his workpeople, and taught by his overlookers, a good deal against the will of most of them. The functions of superintendent were undertaken by Mr. Hardy in person, and when he was present, all went well, but when he was absent—and that happened pretty often—the school became a veritable pandemonium. The scholars mutinied, and the teachers lost their tempers. Forcing his people to attend his own conventicle, and paying them a minimum of wage for a maximum of work, did not tend to make Mr. Hardy either respected or beloved, and as he wended his way homeward on a winter's night, he was often greeted (generally from behind a hedge) with a cry of " Sunday saint, work-day devil." This it was that led to his being called " Saintly Sam," and the nickname stuck.

Another good work which he undertook, or rather promoted, was the building of a new chapel. He subscribed, and persuaded others to subscribe, and, as a further help, offered the stone (at a reduced price) from his own quarry, and engaged to buy the timber at Liverpool, where he bought his own, and so saved a dealer's profit. But a jealous and disappointed contractor, who had a good head for figures, and a shrewd knowledge of prices, protested, one night in the " Cock " bar, and offered to prove, that

Sam had put the dealer's profit into his own pocket, and made a good thing out of the stone. The saint, when he heard of it, denied the imputation, but a good many people did not believe him, and there was a terrible rumpus among the chapel folks, ending in a serious split. After an angry war of words, out of which Mr. Hardy did not come with flying colours, he went over, bag and baggage, to the enemy, or as they put it in Calder, he "turned Church."

The event caused as much excitement in the town as a contested election, and Mr. Balmaine, on the principle of rejoicing more over one repentant sinner than over ninety-and-nine just men, received Saintly Sam with open arms and made much of him in every way.

With the proverbial zeal of a new convert, Mr Hardy became as strenuous a supporter of the Church as he had previously been of Dissent; and, to "make things look fuller," as Bob Rogers said, or out of pure spite, as his former co-religionists averred, he followed up his change of creed with a change of politics. His secession played havoc with the Liberal party. At the preceding election they had returned their man by a majority of ten votes; at the next the Tories won by a majority of fifty, for Saintly Sam had many electors in his employ, and their suffrages, as well as those of his tenants, were always at his disposal.

6*

The Rector could not, of course, do otherwise than offer hospitality to his new convert (whose change of politics, as he flattered himself, was due to his influence). He invited him to dinner, and Sam asked Mr. and Mrs. Balmaine to tea. In this way, a certain friendship was established between the two families, but their ideas and ideals were too divergent for them ever to become intimate. Sam could talk about little else but business; and his wife, who was not a lady, had hardly a thought beyond her house and her children.

The loss of fortune and position did not deprive the Balmaines of any friends they cared to keep; and as for the Hardys, they showed so much sympathy, that Cora, though she could not " cotton " to them, thought better of the Saintly Sams than she had ever thought before. To give Sam his due, he rather liked to be magnanimous when it cost him nothing, and he gave Alfred much fatherly advice, and asked him often to his house. In other days the young fellow would probably have accepted neither Mr. Hardy's patronage nor his invitations. Seeing, however, that Mr. Hardy was one of Calder's biggest men, and the most influential members of the party of which the *Mercury* was the organ, Balmaine found it expedient to accept both, and to treat his host with a great deal more respect than the latter deserved.

CHAPTER XI.

LIZZIE HARDY.

Now it so happened that Mr. Hardy possessed a daughter, who, a few months before the meeting at the " Cock," had rounded off her education at a flashy finishing school in the neighbourhood of London. Lizzie was about nineteen. She had a shapely figure and a pretty face, large brown eyes and pink cheeks, well-cut lips, and a *nez retroussé*, a shallow nature, and a head full of romantic notions. She read three novels a week (not always of the right sort), besides sundry serial stories, and was quite ready to fall in love with any suitable hero whom destiny might throw in her way. Destiny threw in her way Alfred Balmaine, and he seemed to be endowed with every qualification she could desire or that a model lover ought to possess. He was poor (she hated the sordid rich), handsome (she could not bear ugly people), of gentle birth (the Balmaines were one of the oldest families in the county), and a writer (she adored literary men). So she decided to fall in love with Alfred, and without much effort succeeded in conceiving for him a strong fancy, if not a really warm affection. But she had studied her favourite romances too closely not to know how a heroine should behave, and she tried, not unsuccessfully, to let her preference be felt rather than seen. Alfred thought her a very nice girl, and as he had a great liking for music and she was a clever performer on the piano, he began to call at Waterfall House (as Mr. Hardy called his place) rather oftener than he need have done. Cora judged Lizzie less favourably; thought her designing and insincere, and said so; but Alfred ascribed the remark to prejudice and want of knowledge, and its effect was to make him think more about Miss Hardy than before. As time went on, it more than once occurred to him that the pleasure which she seemed to take in his company might be due to something more than mere liking; but the idea, though flattering to his self-esteem, did not take root in his mind. Miss Hardy was not of a sort to fall in love with a poor man; and even if the way were made smooth for him, he did not feel that he should like to become Saintly Sam's son-in-law. All this time Lizzie was studying him like a book, and though he was much slower in succumbing than she expected, she was quite confident of bringing him eventually to her feet and playing a leading part in one of those scenes which she had so often in imagination rehearsed.

At length her opportunity came. She and Alfred were asked to a picnic. Cora had also been invited,

but she did not like picnics, and sent an excuse.
Had she gone she might have saved her cousin some
embarrassment and no little anxiety.

The scene of the picnic was in a romantic valley,
through which ran a swift river, bounded on one
side by wooded heights, on the other by green
meadows. There were the usual *al fresco* banquet,
the usual dancing and champagne drinking, and a
good deal of fun and laughter. Lizzie looked re-
markably well, and was more than ordinarily affable.
Once, when she and Alfred were whirling round in
a galop, he (quite involuntarily, as he thought)
squeezed both her hand and her waist more than
was absolutely necessary. The pressure of his hand
was returned, and when he looked down at her face
her eyes drooped, and a bright tell-tale blush
mantled her cheeks. How pretty she looked! For
the first time he felt himself in danger of falling in
love; and if circumstances had been different—if
that scoundrel Bradley had not robbed his father,
and Saintly Sam had not been hers, he might have
yielded to the impulse. But prudence and conscience bade him beware, and he was careful not to
squeeze his partner's hand a second time.

After the dance a walk in the wood was proposed. When they were half way through, drops
of rain began to fall, the trees swayed ominously to
and fro, and a loud peal of thunder roused the echoes
and startled the ladies. Then followed a general

stampede for the nearest shelter, as to the exact locality of which nobody seemed quite sure. Some ran one way, some another, and by the merest chance Balmaine and Miss Hardy found themselves running in the same direction.

"Where shall we go, Mr. Balmaine; where shall we go?" cried Lizzie.

"I think we had better get back to the 'Rowsley Arms,' and unless I am mistaken, it is nearer this way than by the footpath."

"Oh, but I shall be quite wet through, and I am so much afraid of the thunder. Can we not shelter somewhere? Oh, did you see that flash?"

"Perhaps we shall come across a farm-house or a labourer's cottage. Let us run as fast as we can. Take my arm."

"I am afraid I could not run as fast then. Would you mind giving me your hand?"

Alfred gave her his hand.

"It is good fun after all," she exclaimed merrily; "don't you think so?"

"Do you like it?"

"Yes; don't you?"

"Certainly;" and he did rather, though he was not without misgiving as to what might come of it all.

"Is not that a cottage?"

"It looks like one."

"It is one; don't you see the walls?"

It was a ruined keeper's cottage, picturesquely situated in a glade of the wood; and though the walls were bare and the roof had fallen in, there was a dry corner where one, and possibly two, could comfortably shelter. But it was a very little corner, and when Alfred had arranged a seat for Lizzie he moved a little on one side.

The rain came down more heavily.

"Oh, Mr. Balmaine," exclaimed Lizzie looking up, "you are getting wet; won't you sit down?"

"There is no room, and if I do get a little wet it does not matter."

"It matters a great deal, and there is room; look here;" and she drew aside her skirts and shrank into a smaller compass. "I should be sorry for you to get wet."

Alfred, feeling that it would be ungracious to refuse so kind an invitation, sat down on the log, but it was so tight a squeeze that he had to put his right arm behind her, and her head almost touched his shoulder.

A decidedly dangerous position for an unsophisticated young fellow with a soft heart and a weakness for a pretty face! And Lizzie looked particularly piquant just then. Her cheeks were flushed with exercise, her eyes bright with excitement, and a stray lock which had escaped from its fastening floated across Alfred's shirt-front, and even brushed against his beard.

"Suppose some of the others should come here and surprise us!" was his thought.

"He must pop now. I wonder how he will do it?" was hers.

Then followed a rather long silence, which was broken by Lizzie asking Alfred if he had enjoyed himself.

"Awfully," was his reply.

"I am so glad," she murmured; "I have enjoyed it too. I do not think I ever enjoyed a picnic so much. That run through the wood was so exciting and this old cottage is so romantic."

Alfred said something, but his answer was drowned in a terrific peal of thunder and a frightened scream.

"Oh, Mr. Balmaine!" and if his arm had not promptly encircled her waist Lizzie must have fallen backward on the grass. Her eyes closed, and with a deep-drawn sigh her head dropped on his shoulder. Her cheeks were blanched, for though the faint was a feint the fear was real.

Alfred never exactly knew what he said or how it came about, but the next moment Lizzie was clinging round his neck, whispering how happy he had made her and how much she loved him. His heart was touched and his *amour propre* flattered, and he felt that he could do nothing less than return her embrace and press his lips to hers.

"Dear Alfred," she murmured, "you love me.

What happiness! But—but we'll keep it a secret ; we won't tell anybody yet."

" Not even your father and mother ? "

" Oh, no. I am afraid that papa might be disagreeable. And it will be ever so much nicer and more romantic, don't you think, to keep our engagement a secret ? "—and deceive them all, she was going to add, but an instinctive feeling that the suggestion might not commend itself to her lover arrested the words on her lips.

This was a relief to Alfred, for although he did not like concealments, he shrank from asking Saintly Sam for permission to court his daughter. Though poor he could not forget he was a Balmaine ; to sue for the hand of a vulgar manufacturer's daughter would not be pleasant ; to be refused would be bitter humiliation.

" As you like," he said. " I shall not mention it to your father until you are willing that I should."

" Nor to anybody else."

" Nor to anybody else ; and it is only fair that I should tell you now that I am not in a position to marry, nor for a long time to come, likely to be. My salary is very small, and I have to share it with my mother and aunt."

" How noble of you ! But that is nothing ; we can wait ; and if you leave it to me to manage papa, I am sure he will do something for us."

In her heart she did not believe he would do anything of the sort, and Alfred thought that almost any alternative would be preferable to living on Mr. Hardy's bounty; but not wanting to hurt Lizzie's feelings, he kept this thought to himself, and returned an irrelevant answer.

By this time the storm had begun to abate, and shortly afterwards the rain ceased, and shouts were heard in the near distance.

" We must not let them find us together," cried Lizzie, starting up. " I will go to them, and you can join us in a few minutes."

No sooner said than done. She went one way, he another; and nobody either suspected that they had been together or asked awkward questions.

As Alfred wandered through the wood alone, thinking over the events of the day, he felt anything but satisfied with himself, and subsequent reflection served but to deepen his discontent. It was not merely that long engagements were proverbially objectionable, and for all that appeared to the contrary, years might elapse before he could afford to keep a wife; his first duty was to his mother and to Cora, whose fortune had gone down in the general wreck. Circumstanced as they were, it seemed selfish and almost cruel for him, the stay and support of the family, even to think of marrying. The very fact that he was engaged, when it became known, would, he felt sure, be a new source of anxiety both to his cousin and his mother. Even if there were no other

objection—if his income were multiplied by ten—
they could neither approve of his choice nor of the
Hardy connection. If he had a real love for Lizzie,
such love as he had heard and read of, this objection might not amount to much; they would
waive it for his sake. But he could neither deny to
them nor hide from himself that his fancy was far
from being an absorbing passion. He had yielded
to a momentary impulse, and he had an unpleasant
sense—which, however, he soon dismissed as an un-
generous suspicion—that Lizzie had twisted a few
hasty words into an avowal which deliberately and
in cool blood he would never have made.

Of a surety he had not done wisely. Some may
use a stronger word and say that he acted like a fool.
If he had been older or less impulsive he would probably have told Lizzie that she had made a mistake.
If he had been less scrupulous he would have got
out of the difficulty by ignoring the incident—said
nothing more about it either to Lizzie or to anybody
else. But Balmaine, though he was a young man,
had old-fashioned ideas. He held that a promise
once given, even by implication—above all to a
woman—should be faithfully observed, and this
method of extrication never so much as occurred to
him. Lizzie loved him; and he had led her, or allowed
her to believe, that he loved her. That was enough.
To say now that he did not love her would be both
cruel and unmanly.

All this came to pass only about a month before
Alfred heard of the situation in Switzerland, and
though in the interval he received a good many
letters from Lizzie, and answered some of them, and
they had several times met, they had not yet been
able to contrive a second *téte-à-téte*.   Although his
frequent visits to Waterfall House had begun to
excite some remark, nobody suspected that they
were secretly engaged, but a mistake of Lizzie's revealed their secret to Cora.   She inadvertently put
a letter intended for him into an envelope addressed
to her.

So Alfred had to make a clean breast of it.

Cora was terribly annoyed ; but after the first outburst she said very little, showing only by an occasional remark, either sarcastic or sorrowful, how
deeply she was vexed and grieved.   If the *fiancée*
had been worthy of her cousin, some sweet girl
whom she could have taken to her heart and cherished
as a sister, she would not have cared—would have
been rather pleased, in fact—for, like all true
hearted women, she took a warm interest in lovers'
troubles and thought none the worse of a man for
cherishing an imprudent passion.   But Lizzie
Hardy !   She could not have believed that Alfred
could be such a simpleton.   Her only consolation
was a strong conviction that sooner or later Lizzie
would jilt him.

Not all this did she say to her cousin, but he

. guessed her thoughts, and in one way and another was far from happy. So the chance of going to Switzerland came most opportunely; for though he did not like to say so, there was nothing he so much wanted as to get away from Calder.

CHAPTER XII.

FAREWELLS.

THE confirmation of Balmaine's appointment came sooner than he expected. The proprietors of the *Helvetic News* informed him that, owing to the illness of one of the sub-editors, they were short-handed, and offered, if he would enter on his duties before the end of the month, to pay his travelling expenses to Geneva. That meant in a fortnight, and he resolved to profit by the opportunity. Mr. Grindleton made no difficulty about releasing him, and a week later he had engaged a new editor.

Before this was done Balmaine had informed Lizzie of his approaching departure. In doing so, he laid particular stress on the fact of their engagement, and the necessity thereby laid on him of trying to better himself. While he remained at Calder, he said, there was not the least prospect of his being able to marry, and until he was in a position to keep her as she would like to be kept, without troubling anybody, he could not ask her to be his wife.

This drew from Miss Hardy a letter, in which she said that, although his going away would almost break her heart, she could not deny that he seemed to be acting for the best. She wished him good speed, vowed that she should think of him every minute and pray for him every night, implored him to write to her very, very often, and said so many tender and gracious things that Alfred's heart was touched : he accused himself of misjudging her, and regretted that he could not return her affection with a more ardent love.

An evening or two before he went away he was invited to take tea at Waterfall House. It was a somewhat extensive establishment, about a mile from the town, which Saintly Sam had got as a great bargain, but the outlay in furniture and repairs made it, as he observed to his wife, " a very dear do." It was considered at Calder that Mrs. Hardy had not risen with her husband. This meant that she made no attempt to be other than she ever had been, preferred living in a plain way to inhabiting a grand house, and never looked or felt comfortable either in her carriage or her drawing-room. She was not a little afraid, poor woman, of her stylish daughter, and sometimes wondered how she had come to have such a child, for they did not seem to possess an idea in common. Lizzie detested the kitchen as much as Mrs. Hardy detested the drawing-room, delighted in fine clothes and fine company, and often used language that her mother only half understood. Miss Hardy, on the other hand, found her mother a sore

trouble. She would do servants' work—bake and
cook and make beds—and sometimes when visitors
called, Lizzie found her " throng " in the wash-house.
And then her language! She spoke with a strong
Yorkshire twang, and scattered her aitches about in
lavish profusion. Mr. Hardy was at least consistent
—he had never used the aspirate in his life—but his
wife used it indiscriminately; she could not be
brought to see the difference between an H and any
other letter. When they made calls or received
visitors the daughter passed many a " bad quarter
of an hour," and sometimes almost wished that her
mother would stay in the kitchen altogether.

Saintly Sam, as usual, was very patronising. " I
hope as you'll prosper in your new undertaking,
Balmaine," he observed, as they sat at tea, " and be
a credit to your native place. Everybody thinks
highly of you here. You have edited the *Mercury*
uncommonly well, and your articles have been exten-
sively read. Some folks thought you were too
young; but I did not, and I was never deceived in a
man yet. You were the right man in the right
place, and I am sorry, for th' sake of th' town and
th' cause of loyalty and religion, as you are going
away. That leader of yours, last Saturday, agen th'
Government was a nipper—it was nowt else. It
spoke my mind to a T, and I am seldom wrong
about them things. I hope as th' paper as you are
going to be connected with is on the right side."

" The *Helvetic News* tries to be neutral in politics, I think. At any rate, it does not seem to take strong views either way."

" That's a pity, that's a pity. I like folks to be summat—either fish, flesh, fowl, or good red herring. You know what they're made on then. Everybody knows I am a Conservative. I belonged to th' tother side once, its true ; but what could you expect ? I was brought up Liberal, and most folks sticks to the faith of their fathers, both in politics and religion. There's very few as thinks for themselves, but I did ; and I am of opinion as I came to a right conclusion."

" You were a long time about it, though," thought Balmaine, who was no great admirer of the " prop of his party," as Mr. Hardy was designated at Calder.

" And it's pretty generally known now what my sentiments is," continued Saintly Sam, with much complacency, " they're them of loyalty and religion —our beloved Bible and our revered Queen, as Mr. Pyke said last Sunday—and I command eighty votes in this 'ere borough. You uphold 'em, Mr. Balmaine, and keep the Sabbath, and you'll prosper. It is to keeping the Sabbath as I owe my success in life more than to owt else, I do believe. And we shall always take a warm interest in your welfare, wherever you are ; shall not we, Jane ? "

" That we shall," said Mrs. Hardy heartily. " I

7*

always thinks well of young men as is good to their mothers. You'll ten to one be living in lodgings where you're going to, Mr. Balmaine."

"Certainly," answered Alfred with a smile, "and a pretty cheap lodging, too. An hotel would be quite beyond my means."

"Lodgings or hothels, they're all the same. You'll have to see as your bed sheets is not damp, or you'll be getting your death. Many a one has got their death by sleeping in a damp bed. My poor brother Tom did. He took a rheumatic fever, was in a hagony three weeks and died skryking."

"Screaming, mother," put in Lizzie indignantly, "why will you use that horrid word?"

"Mr. Balmaine knows what I mean, and I never could talk fine. I mun ayther talk my own way or howd my tongue. Mind what I say about damp beds, Mr. Balmaine, and take warning by my brother Tom. And always count your shirts and things when they comen home fro' th' wash, or else you'll be losing summat. Some o' them strange washer-women is most terrible rogues, not to speyk of knocking your things i' pieces and burning 'em into rags wi' chemic."

Lizzie looked daggers, but fearing that if she spoke she might make matters worse, she averted her gaze from Alfred and, as her mother would have said, "held her noise."

"Here's a bit of a present as I've bought for you,

if you'll kindly accept it," Mrs. Hardy went on ; "it is a housewife, and you'll happen find it useful o'er yon. There's needles int', and there's pins int', and a thimble and a bit o' cotton and a twothry shirt buttons. There'll ten to one be nobody to mend you where you're going to, and you'll find it handy if you want to stitch a button on your shirt or mend a rent i' your trousers."

" Mother ! " shrieked Lizzie, her face aflame, and almost choking with shame and vexation.

" Well, what is it, child ? " said Mrs. Hardy looking innocently at her daughter. " What have I said wrong this time ? "

" Nothing at all, I am sure," interposed Alfred. " Thank you very much, Mrs. Hardy. You are very kind, and I have no doubt I shall find the housewife exceedingly useful."

" You'll be getting a wife yourself one of these days," said Saintly Sam, with a laugh at his own joke. " I like young fellows to get wed—it steadies 'em. You look out for a wife, Balmaine."

" I must first make my fortune, Mr. Hardy, or, at any rate, an income sufficient to keep a wife."

" You must marry a girl with an income, that's what you must do—not with an income to come, but an income as has come. Marrying a forten is th' finest way of making money I know—you make so much in one day. And that reminds me of th' forten as us Hardys is after. It looks decidedly hopeful. I really begin to believe we shall get it, after all."

"I thought you believed that already, Mr. Hardy?"

"So I did, so I did," replied Saintly Sam, rather confusedly; "but there is degrees, you know, there is degrees, and I believe in it now more than ever. All the shares is taken up, and we have got power to issue another thousand, so we shall not want for powder and shot. And that is not all. Ferret has heard of an old fellow at Halifax—he left this country thirty years since—as saw John Hardy in London about ten or fifteen years after he left Calder, saw him and spoke to him. He was then partner in the firm of Birkdale, Bickerdyke, and Hardy, of which he afterwards became the head."

"How is it that old fellow you speak of did not mention the fact sooner?"

"Hardy asked him not, and the thing passed out of his mind till t' other day, when somebody here as he is akin to sent him word about the meeting at the 'Cock.' Ferret thinks it very important, and he is going over to Halifax express to see Murgatroyd —that's the old fellow's name. He's very full of it, Ferret is."

"Very important evidence, I should say," observed Alfred carelessly; "supposing Philip Hardy and his daughter are really dead."

"Dead! why they are as dead as door-nails; they

must be dead," returned Saintly Sam, almost angrily
The suggestion that either the missing heir or
heiress might possibly still be living made him
quite angry. "No no my lad, that would never
do, to go and spend a mint of money and then
one of 'em to turn up and bag the lot. Them two
millions must come to Calder, Mr. Balmaine—and
will. I mean to go on with this job and I never
yet failed in owt as I undertook."

Alfred wondered what his host would say if he
knew that Warton and himself were engaged in an
attempt to find either Philip Hardy or Vera, and
how a revelation of the fact would affect his relations with Lizzie.

Shortly afterwards he took his leave. When he
shook hands with Lizzie she gave him a significant
look. It had been arranged that they should meet
for a farewell interview in a sequestered part of the
grounds, and Alfred, instead of passing out by the
lodge gates, turned aside and went by a devious path
to keep his tryst.

He had not been there long when Lizzie came
running.

"I have not many minutes to spare," she said
breathlessly, and then she threw her arms round
Alfred's neck and fell a-weeping, for albeit she
consciously posed as an afflicted heroine, and rather
over-did the part, she cared so much for Balmaine
just then, or thought she did, that his departure was

a real grief to her. "You will write to me very often," she whispered as they were about to separate; "and—and I hope you will excuse my mother. It is her way. She means no harm."

The remark was indiscreet; it undid all the effect of her weeping, which so touched Alfred's heart that he had felt for a moment as if he really loved her.

She is ashamed of her mother, he thought. She has a good deal more reason to be ashamed of her father.

The interview lasted only a few minutes, for Lizzie feared that her absence might be remarked. After a few more words and a farewell embrace she ran towards the house, and Alfred leaped over the garden wall into the road.

"Hallo!" cried a voice he knew; "do you always come out of Mr. Hardy's garden that way, Balmaine?"

The speaker was Warton.

"I have done so to-night," said Alfred coolly; "it is rather nearer than round by the lodge gates."

"And less likely to attract attention, I suppose—unless you happen to jump on some unfortunate passer-by, as you nearly did on me just now. However, I have no wish to pry into secrets. A nod is as good as a wink to a blind horse, you know. Has the Saint anything fresh about the fortune?"

Alfred told what had passed.

" I don't think much of that tale," observed the lawyer's clerk. " It's a case of the wish being father to the thought, I expect. And if we cannot find either the girl or her father it makes no odds to us who gets the fortune. But there's no doubt that Hardy is getting hotter. When a man lets his mind dwell on a thing of that sort, he ends by losing his judgment altogether, and becoming as credulous as a gambler. Sam is an uncommonly smart man of business in his own line, but fortune hunting is not in his line, and I should not be a bit surprised if he sacrificed the substance to the shadow—lost one fortune in trying to get another."

" But you said he did not more than half believe in the Hardy fortune."

" I don't think he did at first ; but the hope of pocketing forty thousand pounds is getting the upper hand of his judgment. The gambling spirit in him is roused, and the more money he spends the harder it will be for him to draw back. But never mind Sam, now. Did you get that paper I sent you this morning—your brief in the matter of Philip and Vera Hardy, you know ? "

" I did ; but I have not had time to read it."

" Read it at your leisure. It contains nothing I have not told you before ; and is merely to refresh your memory and serve as a reference when you are over yon. You will see Artful and Higginbottom, of course."

" Of course ; I am too much interested in the case to omit so essential a point."

" All right. And if you keep your wits about you we shall find our heiress before Sam finds the forty thousand he is after. But I must be off : Mary will be wondering what has become of me." And after an exchange of " good nights," the clerk went one way and Balmaine another.

Alfred walked thoughtfully homeward. The conclusion to which Warton had evidently come, that he and Lizzie were courting, did not trouble him much ; the clerk could be trusted to keep his surmises to himself. Alfred's chief present concern referred to his mother and his cousin. Mrs. Balmaine's health was slowly improving, and that was so far satisfactory ; but her mind had not recovered its balance, and her temper was as querulous as ever. A little while ago she had reproached him with want of energy, and told him to follow the example of his brother George, and seek his fortune in a foreign land. She looked upon his connection with the local press as a sort of degradation, and wondered that he should have so little spirit as to accept the wages of a vulgar tradesman like Grindleton ; yet now, when he was actually going away, she said he was deserting her in her old age, and that she should have to end her days in the workhouse. This was hard to bear, but Cora's sympathy and counsel, and his conviction that he was acting for the best, enabled him to bear it with patience ; yet he felt sorry to leave his cousin to sustain the heat and burden of the day alone, and he proposed, in order that she might be free from anxiety as to money, to remit her half his salary. This she positively refused.

"That would leave you only £75 a year," she said ; "and you cannot live at Geneva on £75 a year. We shall manage very well. One hundred and fifty pounds and my literary earnings (proudly) will be quite enough for two women."

Alfred smiled.

"Your literary earnings! You talk as if you were a swell author with a princely income. It will be quite time enough to reckon your literary earnings when you get them. In the meanwhile you must consent to share my literary earnings."

So it was agreed that he should send them £50 a year.

"That will be a fair division," observed Cora. "If you were to send us more it would be unfair, and I will not have anything unfair if I can help it."

CHAPTER XIII.

ARTFUL AND HIGGINBOTTOM.

Mr. Artful, senior member of the firm of Artful and Higginbottom, was a gentleman of sixty, with white silky hair, a complexion like a piece of crumpled brown paper, little keen grey eyes, and a wonderfully urbane manner; almost too urbane in fact, for it was hardly in human nature to take the very close personal interest in his clients and their affairs, which he made it an invariable rule to display. He could scarcely have manifested greater delight at seeing Balmaine if the latter had been a son of his own, upon whom he had not set eyes for many years. He probably saw in him a possible client; and when he learnt the nature of his visitor's business his smiling face was clouded for a moment —but only for a moment—by a slight shade of disappointment.

"Ah, that is it! You want information about Hardy trust. Well, I shall be most happy to tell you anything I know, and if you can help us to find a clue to the fate of Mr. Philip Hardy or his daughter we shall be very much obliged to you. It is a troublesome affair, and the executors, both gentlemen of high position in the city of London, , would be only too glad to get rid of it. It is solely from a sense of duty and a strong conviction that the heir will sooner or later appear, or be heard of, that they refrain from washing their hands of the matter, and asking the Court of Chancery to relieve them of their responsibility, under the Relief of Trustees Act of 1851 ; and unless we have news of Mr. Hardy before very long, say, within a twelve-month, this is the course we shall advise our clients to follow, and then the estate would probably escheat to the Crown. A great pity, but what can we do ? "

" Unless some heir-at-law were to turn up ? "

" Of course ; but so far as we know the late Mr. Hardy had no relatives except his son Philip. Those who knew him best think that he was an illegitimate son, and for that reason kept silence about his origin. If that be so, nobody save his son, or other issue, could inherit. Still, nothing certain is known, and it will, I think, be very difficult for any of the claimants of whom we have heard to prove their relationship to the late John Hardy. As you come from Calder, you, of course, know all about the Hardy Fortune Company (Limited). Very in-genious, I am sure ; and the story of Mr. Hardy's supposed flight from Calder is romantic in the ex-treme, and does Mr. Ferret great credit. But we shall throw no impediments in the way. Let him prove that Philip is dead without issue, and that his father was the veritable John Hardy who ran away from Calder fifty years ago, and the estate will —subject to the sanction of the Court of Chancery —be handed over to his clients. But we are a long way from that yet, Mr. Balmaine."

Alfred thought it best to tell Mr. Artful frankly how he came to be interested in the matter, and why he sought for information.

The lawyer smiled until his little eyes almost disappeared.

" I am very glad to hear it," he exclaimed warmly. " I fancied you might be an emissary from those fortune-hunting people. I know what they say— they say that we want to keep the estate in our own hands (*qui s'excuse s'accuse*, thought Balmaine). It is false, we want to do nothing of the sort. You may depend on our hearty co-operation. I am glad you have taken the matter up. Your connection with the Press will count greatly in your favour. Yes, Philip Hardy was frequently in Switzerland. You may find some trace of him. You will doubtless travel about a good deal, and if you should be successful you may depend on being handsomely remunerated. I do not mean in merely finding Philip Hardy, but in finding a clue to his fate and that of his daughter.

" Do not mistake me, Mr. Artful," said Balmaine, slightly colouring. " I am not an amateur detective. Consider that I take an interest in the case—that is all. I am poor, as I have said, and if I incur expense in my search I will ask you to recoup me. But for myself I do not ask reward ; if, however, anybody should aid me I might ask——"

" Yes, I understand. By-the-bye, you know our theory, that Philip Hardy is immured in some Austrian dungeon, probably in [the North of Italy. If you can throw any light on the mystery we shall be glad, very glad. And now I must pass you on to Mr. Baggs. You will find him in the next room. Good day, sir, good day. I hope you will have a pleasant journey, and return with Mr. Hardy and his daughter."

And Mr. Artful smiled a gracious smile, and bowed a courtly bow.

" Chivalrous young fool," he muttered, as the door closed behind Balmaine, " pretends not to care for money ! "

Baggs was a very pleasant old fellow, and, if possible, more affable than his master ; but he had little to tell Balmaine that the latter did not already know. He showed him copies of Philip Hardy's letters to his father, written out fair in a book which had evidently been frequently consulted. They all referred to business, and contained little more than formal advice of drafts which Philip had passed on his father's firm ; but, as in one or two of them he mentioned having written fully a few days previously, it was evident that their correspondence had not been limited to business communications, and the last of all, dated from Lugano, said that he had just had Vera's photo taken, and would send it in a subsequent letter.

" Have you got this photo of Miss Hardy ? " asked Balmaine.

" I am sorry to say we have not, sir. I question if it ever came. The letter from Lugano, as you will perceive, was written only a few weeks before the old man died, which, as we think, was about the time his son fell into the hands of the Austrians."

" Can you show me the originals of these letters ? "

" Certainly," answered the old clerk, looking somewhat surprised ; " but I assure you they are faithful copies ; not a word has been altered or added."

" I am quite sure of that. I should like to see the originals, nevertheless, if only to acquaint myself with the character of Philip Hardy's handwriting."

" By all means, I will get them."

As he spoke, Mr. Baggs went to a big japanned tin box, marked " John Hardy's Trustees, No. 2," and after fumbling a few minutes among a mass of papers, produced a bundle of dusty letters. They were tied together and carefully docketed, generally with the words, " Philip Hardy, advising draft for £——." All were written on foreign post, and having been folded in the {old-fashioned way, the direction and post-marks were on the outer sheet. They had been posted at sundry places, and showed what a wanderer the man was, and that he had never remained long in the same locality. Although most of them were written in Italy, many were dated from Switzerland, but only two from France, from which Alfred naturally concluded that Philip Hardy's wanderings had been almost altogether limited to the two former countries. One, dated from the Baths of Lucca, mentioned briefly, and in a postscript, the birth of Vera. It was probably written at the time when father and son were estranged, owing to the latter's marriage. The last letter of all, though dated from Pallanza, bore the post-mark of Lugano, and the half-erased imprint of an hotel at Locarno, the Hotel Martino.

Of all these things Balmaine took careful note, especially of the dates of the letters, the places from which they were written, and the names of the bankers or others to whose order Philip Hardy had made his drafts.

"Is there anything more I can do for you?"· asked Baggs, as Alfred closed his memorandum book.

"Yes, tell me what like a man was Philip Hardy when you last saw him."

"That was the last time he was in England, thirteen years ago. Dear me, how time flies! Let me see—yes, I remember him very well. He did not stay very long ; he said he must hurry back his wife and child, whom he had left at—where was it ? Let me see."

"Somewhere in Italy ? " suggested Alfred.

"No, not Italy—Switzerland, near some lake, I think.   There are lakes in Switzerland, I suppose ? "

"Only about a thousand," returned Balmaine gravely.

"Bless me, what a country for water it must be. Well, I cannot for the life of me remember the name of the lake, but I can tell you what Mr. Philip was like.   Height about five feet ten, long-limbed and slim, but strong, I should say, very strong. Laughing blue eyes with long lashes ; I remember telling my wife what beautiful eyes he had.   Light-complexioned, chestnut hair and beard, and a pleasant manner.   We used to say that everybody liked him but his father.   Did not seem to care much about money, as different from the old man as chalk from cheese, and no more idea of business than a child.   Quite a gipsy sort of man.   The father must have wondered—I am sure other people did—how he came to have such a son.   He had out-of-the-way ideas, too, and was always doing out-of-the-way things.   That's why I sometimes think he may still be living in some out-of-the-way place, if not in Europe, then in Asia, Africa, or America."

"I should think that is very likely," observed

Balmaine, amused by this rather comprehensive suggestion.

" Anyhow, sir, I hope you will find either him or the little girl, or ascertain what has become of them."

" I mean to try," said the young fellow, and with that he took his leave.

8*

CHAPTER XIV.

A SUCCESSFUL JOURNALIST.

" WHY am I giving myself so much trouble about this affair ? " was the question Alfred asked himself as he strolled through Lincoln's Inn Fields ; "and why should I take so much interest in the business of people I never saw, probably never shall see ? "

A very pertinent question, to which there was more than one answer.

First of all, from a desire to oblige Warton, who had behaved so well at the time of his father's death, and who, though rather a rough diamond, was a very good fellow. If there was any chance of doing the clerk a good turn—and the finding of the missing Hardys might conceivably put money in his pocket—it was his duty to do it. Warton, moreover, had contrived to communicate to Balmaine some of his own eagerness and enthusiasm, and the latter's curiosity was thoroughly roused. What could have become of Philip Hardy and his daughter ? Had the former, as was surmised, been immured in some Austrian dungeon, or, as was equally possible, if not more probable, shot by order of a drum-head court-

martial? In that case what had become of his
child? Perhaps some good soul had adopted her,
perhaps her mother's relatives (who were her
mother's relatives?) had found her out, and were
bringing her up. It might even be that she was
working for her living, or begging her bread, or
(horrible thought!) trudging through England or
France as the companion of some villainous Italian
organ-grinder. It was conceivable, too, that she
might be living near the fortress in which her father
was confined, waiting patiently for his release.
Hardly probable, however. In that event, Philip
Hardy would surely have communicated with his
friends; he would want money, and he would not
let his child waste her life in the wretched mono-
tony of some Austrian garrison town, away from all
the advantages of education. There were other and
darker possibilities. Italy was not the most secure
of countries, and it was quite conceivable that
Hardy and his daughter might have been murdered
by brigands, drowned in crossing a lake, or de-
stroyed by an avalanche in some Alpine pass.

All these suppositions added piquancy to the
mystery, about which there was enough of romance
to fire his imagination and suggest a great variety
of possible solutions. And what were his chances
of success? He could not think they were very
brilliant, yet he did not despair, and the more he
thought the stronger grew the conviction that,

sooner or later, and somehow or other, he should
find Miss Vera Hardy—if she were alive.

As Balmaine reached this conclusion he arrived at
the office of Mr. Furbey, the newspaper correspondent, to whose influence he was indebted for his
appointment on the editorial staff of the *Helvetic
News*. Furbey was a middle-aged man with long
sandy whiskers tipped with white, a big face, and a
complexion which suggested that he had a weakness
for good living. He dined Alfred at his club and
gave him some good advice.

"It is a queer sort of paper, the *Helvetic News*,"
he said; "it has had some ups and downs already,
and will have more before it has done, I expect."

"Before it has done!" exclaimed Balmaine, looking rather unpleasantly surprised. I hope you don't
think it is near its latter end."

"No, not quite so bad as that. Before its prosperity is really assured, I ought to have said; for I
have seen so many papers start up and go down that
I am never quite sure about anything that has not
three or four years behind it, and not always then.
But just now the *Helvetic* seems to be in very good
feather. I get my cheque every month, and I used
to be glad to get it every three. It is by no means
a bad opening, if you want to acquire experience in
your profession."

"That I do, most decidedly. But there is one
thing that has rather been weighing on my mind

—do you think I shall be able to do the work ? "

" Of sub-editing the *Helvetic News?*" said Furbey with an amused laugh. " Of course, you will. You are too modest, Mr. Balmaine. Why, I do not think there is a pressman in Fleet Street who would not undertake to edit the *Times* at a minute's notice, with the full belief that he could do it better than Delane himself. But you will mend of that—modesty and journalism are a contradiction in terms. If you want to get on you must assert yourself. It did not use to be so, but the most important qualifications of a journalist now-a-days are impudence and push."

" In that case I am afraid I shall not become an ornament of my profession, for I fear that I am sadly lacking in both these qualifications."

" Most men are at starting, and you have not had much chance of developing either impudence or push down there at Calder. You will find your work at Geneva a good deal more interesting, I fancy, than chronicling small beer at Calder.

Alfred winced. He did not like this belittling of the paper he had edited and the place where he was born.

" Don't be vexed," continued Furbey, who had detected the young fellow's annoyance. " You will be of the same opinion yourself before we meet again. I have gone through the same thing myself.

I received my first training in the office of a Catholic paper in the south of Ireland."

"You are an Irishman then ? "

" I am, or as I once heard a countryman of mine say, who had been a long time settled in England, I was originally. Well, when I was about twenty I went north, and got a berth on a Tory Protestant paper in Belfast, and one of the first jobs I had was reporting the speeches of a lot of Presbyterian parsons at a religious meeting. You may imagine my feelings. But it was a useful experience. It taught me a lesson in tolerance I shall never forget. I learnt for the first time in my life that there are two sides even to a religious question, and now I have no religious opinion left worth mentioning.

" And does your indifferentism extend to politics ? "

" I am a Liberal if anything; most pressmen are I fancy. But I cannot afford to let my political opinions interfere with my professional duties."

" You mean that you are for the side that pays the best? " said Alfred with a slight touch of scorn in his voice.

" I mean that if I was offered a berth—and wanted one—on the staff of a Tory paper I should take it, and write what I was told to write. You are shocked, I dare say; but that is a feeling you will get over by-and-by. Do you think the fellows who do the leaders in the dailies believe one half they write? They are not such fools."

" They are not high-principled journalists, then,"
was Balmaine's thought, but not wanting to offend
his host he said, " Perhaps you are right as to your
facts—though I confess I am very much surprised
—but can a man heartily and effectively advocate a
cause in which he does not believe ? "

" Certainly. You know the *True Blue* ? "

Alfred knew it very well. The *True Blue* had
been his father's favourite weekly paper, and he
used often to call attention to the vigour of its
literary style, and the soundness of its political
views."

" Well, I know the editor of it, and a very clever
fellow he is, but a Radical and Freethinker."

" Am I to understand, then, that London journalists
as a class are ready to prostitute their pens to the
highest bidder ? "

" You put the case too strongly. All that I say
is, that most pressmen, being dependent on their
pens for their daily bread, cannot be choosers ; they
must take such situations as they can get, and
write—if it be their function to do original articles
—what they are ordered to write. I get my living
by writing London letters for country papers. I
work with the advertising agent whose name is
over the door. You know the arrangement. We
give a letter a week for a column of space, which
my colleague fills with advertisements, and between
us we make a very fair thing of it. The letters I

write are, of course, pretty much alike as regards
gossip, but when I touch on politics or political
personages I must, of course, adapt my remarks to
my audience."

" Which means, I suppose," laughed Balmaine,
" that when you write for the *Calder Mercury* you
praise up Disraeli as a heaven-born statesman, while
in the *Bradford Blazer* you denounce him as an
unscrupulous charlatan."

" No, no ; I never use unparliamentary language.
I don't think it pays. But don't you think that
promiscuous advocacy is far worse that mercenary
journalism ? Whether this or that government is
the better: whether this or that measure is wise or
expedient, is merely a matter of opinion ; whether
you are right or wrong nobody is much the worse ;
and whatever you may yourself think, your paper,
at least, has the courage of its convictions, and, as a
rule, sticks to the side in which it professes to believe. But a barrister is always ready, for a certain
number of guineas, to plead for a murderer or de-
fend an oppressor of the poor. Advocacy is the most
immoral of professions. Nothing would persuade
me to become a barrister, yet barristers are esteemed
honourable men, and the one who most success-
fully perverts justice and prostitutes his talent becomes the keeper of the Queen's conscience and a
great peer."

" You forget," said Balmaine, surprised alike by

Furbey's views and by the bitterness with which he expressed them: " you forget that unless both sides of a contested case are effectually stated essential facts may be forgotten, important considerations overlooked. And how is a barrister to know before-hand that a client is in the wrong—how, until he has heard what the other side has to say, know the weakness of his own ? "

" To such cases as that my remarks do not apply; but there are cases in which counsel must know that they are pleading for an unrighteous cause, and that they can win only by imputing baseness to their opponents and practically bearing false witness against their neighbours, and yet if they do win they get high praise and more business."

" But don't you see that if the law be right in regarding an accused person as innocent until he is proved to be guilty, advocates cannot be wrong in acting on the same principle? There is something in what you say—the system has its drawbacks; there are unscrupulous barristers, as well as un-scrupulous journalists, but taking it all round you must admit that it does not work badly."

" I admit nothing of the sort," said Furbey, thumping his fist on the table; " I would abolish it utterly. But let us drop the subject; it always puts me out of temper. I think I did not tell you that the editor of the *Helvetic News* is a connection of mine, a half-cousin in fact."

"No, I was not aware. Mr. Gibson, you mean. I have had a letter from him."

"Yes, I mean Mr. Gibson; Ned Gibson, we generally call him. I will write and ask him to do for you what he can. He is a very decent fellow, as you will find; but he has his fads, as you will also find. He fancies he has an awful lot of work to do, and it is to that idea, I imagine, that your engagement is partly due. He pretends to want more help. Why, I could edit that paper on my head. I do almost as much work in a day as he does in a week. But you keep in with him; he may be very useful to you. Another thing; if you keep your eyes open you may fake up a letter now and again for one of the London papers."

"Yes," said Balmaine, to whom the idea was by no means new, "I intend to do so. Which of them would you recommend me to try?"

"I really cannot tell you. One is about as good as another, I fancy, for your purpose. Try one, and if that is no go, try another. You should not have much difficulty in writing something worth printing. Accounts of Alpine accidents, especially if the victims happen to be English travellers, always make good copy. I should think you might easily pick up fifty or sixty pounds a year in that way."

"I am afraid that is too good to be true," said Alfred; "but I shall do my best, and you may be

sure that if I fail it will not be for want of perseverance."

Fifty pounds, or even half of it, would make a
nice addition to his slender income, and without
some such help it would be impossible for him to do
much towards solving the Hardy mystery. He felt
encouraged by Furbey's opinion that he should be
able to do so well, but for the rest, the conversation
had been rather an unpleasant surprise. He was
disillusioned. He had thought that London
journalists were a class apart; that the men who
every morning weigh statesmen in the balance and
instruct the nation in its duties—who write as if
their judgment were faultless and their knowledge
unlimited—were of a morality beyond reproach, and
would rather perish than express opinions which
they did not entertain or advocate a cause in which
they did not believe. But if Furbey was right
their knowledge was empiricism, their morality a
fraud, and their opinions a pretence. He could not
credit it. Furbey was a cynic, and thought that
others were as destitute of professional honour as
himself. At any rate, if journalists were no better
than their kind they were surely no worse, and there
must be among them men who would scorn to say
what they did not think, and rather starve than
prostitute their pens for money and place.

CHAPTER XV.

A LARGE room on the first floor of a house in a leading street of Geneva, known as "La Rue de la Montagne." Though lofty and well lighted, this room is of somewhat barn-like aspect and barely furnished. There is neither carpet on the floor nor paper on the walls. In the centre is a big table littered with unopened journals in various tongues. In the neighbourhood of the windows are three small writing-tables and as many chairs. What the original colour of them may have been it would be hard to say, but they are now black with ink stains and polished with much usage.

At one of the tables sits a man busily writing; as it would seem from frequent references to a foreign journal before him, translating. At another table sits another man: with a big pair of scissors he makes cuttings from an English newspaper and with a big brush pastes them on a sheet of foolscap. When he has done with the newspaper he drops it on the floor, and as there are about fifty papers there already he looks as if he were being gradually engulphed in a sea of news, or preparing to make a holocaust of himself, for a spark from the cigar he is smoking would almost certainly set the pile in a blaze.

The room is the sub-editors' den of the *Helvetic News*, and the two men are the sub-editors. For some time neither of them looks up, the only sounds heard being the scratching of the pen and the click of the scissors. They are " making copy " with an industry begotten of the consciousness that it is wanted, and that they are rather behind with their work.

A knock at the door.

" That will be Lud," says the scissors-and-paste man. " Have you any copy ready, Milnthorpe? *Entrez!* "

Whereupon there enters a stout, good-looking young fellow in a drab blouse. He has a pleasant smile and holds in his hand a number of printed slips.

" *Bonjour, messieurs*," says Lud, as he goes briskly up to the scissors-and-paste man's desk.

" This is what I have over, Mr. Delane," he says in very fair English, at the same time showing his slips.

" Why, what a lot you have ! Chauncy's letter, too, that Mr. Gibson said had to go in anyhow. My eye, won't there be a row ! "

Another knock at the door, followed by the

entrance of the knocker, a tall, well set-up man, with a game leg and a walking-stick.

After casting an angry glance at Lud, as the latter withdraws, he greets the sub-editors with easy familiarity and seats himself unceremoniously on the big table.

The new-comer may be twenty-eight or thirty years old; he has well-cut features and a healthy complexion, albeit the squareness of his jaws and the thinness of his lips, which are unadorned by beard or moustache, give him a somewhat hard, and, at times, a cynical expression. His brown hair is closely cropped, and his general appearance that of a man who has undergone military training.

"Any news?" he says, drawing a cigar-case from his pocket. "I'll thank you for a light, Delane."

"Nothing very important, I think. Have you brought any copy with you?"

"Of course I have; that is what I came for. Here it is. Give it to Lud yourself. If he mauls any more of my copy, as he did last week, I'll wring his neck for him."

"I would not try anything of that sort on if I were you, Corfe. Lud is a sturdy fellow, and not so much to blame as you think. His compositors don't know a word of English, remember."

"I know that; but you forget that I both corrected the proof and looked over the revise. If the mistake had occurred in the text I should not have cared ; but to see an article you have taken pains with headed 'A Remarkable Rope,' instead of 'A Remarkable Pope,' is more than flesh and blood can stand. I cannot go to the Café du Roi without somebody asking me if I have not got a bit of that remarkable rope in my pocket. Nothing will persuade me that Lud did not do it on purpose, and, by gad, I'll be even with him. Has the new boy come?"

"You mean Balmaine. He was to come last night, but I have not seen him yet. I suppose he would first pay his respects to Leyland and Mayo in the office below."

"Do you know anything of him?"

"Nothing ; except that he has been on a country paper."

"They should have given me that place."

"You don't know German, and they want somebody who does."

"German is not so necessary as they make out, and I would have undertaken to learn it, and I know Italian. But Mayo is no friend of mine, nor Gibson either."

"Hush! that is Gibson's step on the stairs."

Whereupon Delane betakes himself to his scissors and paste, Corfe becomes absorbed in a copy of the *Journal de Lacustrie,* and silence reigns once more. The next moment the door opens again and the editor-in-chief, followed by Balmaine, advances into the room.

" Let me introduce you to your new colleague— Mr. Balmaine," he says, after an exchange of greetings.

Whereupon Alfred is presented in form to Delane and Milnthorpe and to Mr. Corfe, "one of our contributors."

" Any letters for me ? " asks the editor.

" You will find several in your room," says Delane.

" Has Lud plenty of copy ? "

" Enough for the present, and we are making more. What time will your leader be ready, Mr. Gibson ? "

" I have not thought of a subject yet. About six o'clock, I hope. Will you step this way, Balmaine ? "

As the editor spoke he opened an inner door, which led into his own sanctum. It was much better furnished than the sub-editors' apartment. The chairs, as well as Mr. Gibson's desk, were of mahogany ; there was a well-filled bookcase, and, ranged in a long rack, were files of the *Helvetic News* and of several English and other journals.

" I am glad you called on me first," said the editor, a big-boned middle-aged man, with an intelligent and kindly, though not very well favoured face, as he glanced through his letters. " It is always pleasanter to be introduced than to introduce yourself. You were not aware, I suppose, that we had got a second sub-editor ? "

"No; the last I heard was that you were short-handed."

"So we were. Delane and I had to do all the work, and at the best I have my hands quite full. This is a very arduous position, Mr. Balmaine— a very arduous position, full of anxiety; and the worst of it is that I hardly ever get a moment's leisure,—so very much to do." (Alfred thought of Furbey.) "Now you have come I shall not be so tied. But I have not told you about Milnthorpe. He came here a fortnight since, poor devil, begging for something to do. I felt really sorry for him and persuaded Leyland and Mayo to let me try him as second sub-editor, at thirty francs a week—that is all he gets—thirty francs a week. And he is really working very well, translates with facility, and seems to have that journalistic instinct without which nobody can become a pressman worth his salt, let his other qualifications be what they may. And now about your own work. You will look through the German and the German-Swiss papers and turn into English whatever you may find suitable, boiling down or padding out at your own discretion. You have studied the paper, of course?"

"Of course, Mr. Gibson."

"Well, you will see the style of thing we want. The details—the make-up of the paper and so forth —you had better leave to Mr. Delane; he is a very

9*

clever young fellow and I want you to work with him. You understand ? "

"Perfectly."

"And do you think you will be able to do me an occasional leader or leaderet ? "

"I think so. I will do my best."

"Thank you. It would be a great relief. You have no idea how much I have to do. When you see your way to a subject let me know. As to politics, we ought to be neutral, but at present our proclivities are Liberal."

"At present ? " said Balmaine with a smile.

"Yes," returned the editor gravely. "I said it advisedly, for a short time ago our proclivities were Conservative, and for ought I know they may be Conservative again. Leyland and Mayo, our proprietor and his manager, are sometimes hardish up —this is, of course, in confidence, though you will probably find it out soon enough yourself—and require financial help. In plain English, they have to raise the wind, and we trim our political sails so as to catch, or shall I say encourage, the favouring breeze. We are trimming just now. Our financial ally—I ought almost to say co-proprietor, for I am by no means sure that he has not bought a share— is an American banker, who lately opened an office here and is carrying all before him—a man of immense energy. He is a Liberal—all Americans are, I think—and for that reason we are rather patting Liberalism on the back. Three months ago we were doing the other thing."

" I understand," said Alfred gravely, though inwardly much amused ; " and yourself, Mr. Gibson, are you Conservative or Liberal ? "

" Neither, or both—just as you like to put it. In other words, I am a Liberal-Conservative, and I make a point of avoiding extremes. It is bad policy for a paper like ours to take strong party views. However, as we make a speciality of social and continental subjects, you will have plenty of scope without touching on politics, and I shall do all the political leaders myself."

" I think that is about all I have to say at present," resumed the editor, wetting his pen and shuffling his " copy " paper, as if he had hit upon a suitable subject for a leader and was anxious to begin. " There is no hurry about seeing Leyland and Mayo to-day ; I will introduce you to them to-morrow. By-the-bye, I forgot to ask you how Kit was looking. I have not seen him for an age."

" Kit ? "

" I mean my kinsman, Kit Furbey."

" I thought he was looking very well, and he seemed to be in excellent spirits."

" And well he may be. He makes a capital thing out of that letter-writing business, and with very little exertion, too. I wish I had such a nice easy job.   Did he say anything about law and lawyers ? "

" Rather.   He said a good deal."

" Denounced all lawyers as rogues and vagabonds, and called English law an ungodly tangle, didn't he ? " said Gibson with a laugh.   " He always does ; do you know why ? "

" I suppose because he thinks so."

" Very likely he does ; but he did not always.   It is not very long since he wanted to be a barrister himself.   After eating a lot of dinners and paying a lot of fees, he got ignominiously plucked—twice over.   What could you expect ?   He would not work, and when he wanted his fees back—something like forty pounds, I think—they would not give 'em him.   And now he never loses an opportunity of abusing lawyers and all their works. Rather absurd, you know, for everybody knows about the plucking.   Still, Kit is a very decent fellow, and always ready—God bless me, what is that ? "

" That " was a tremendous uproar in the next room, whither the editor, followed by Balmaine, excitedly rushed.   Delane had set his newspapers in a blaze, and he and Milnthorpe were trying to stamp the fire out, looking, as they danced among the flames, like a couple of lunatics.   Corfe was making play with his stick, but taking care, as Alfred noticed, not to go near enough to hurt himself. Gibson trampled among the burning embers like a hero, and his feet being of abnormal size, the fire was soon got under, but not until the pile of journals had been reduced to charred morsels.

"Now, look there, Delane," said Gibson, as soon as he recovered his wind, "no more smoking, if you please ; at any rate, when you are making copy. It is a wonder you were not burnt to death. Send for the boy to clear up the mess."

Delane looked very wild and a good deal scared. He could hardly be more than twenty, and was decidedly good-looking—curly black hair and a silky moustache, a dark oval face, and deep blue eyes with long lashes. Milnthorpe was at least ten years older, light-complexioned and lantern-jawed, and his long serious face was so rarely relaxed by a smile that Delane, who, like so many other journalists, was an Irishman, had christened him the "Knight of the Rueful Countenance."

"A dear smoke, that," said Delane, looking sadly at his foot gear as Gibson withdrew to his own room. "Spoiled me a new pair of boots. They cost me eighteen francs only last week. That would keep me in *Veveys fins* for a twelvemonth— four a penny, aren't they, Corfe ? "

"You ought to know better than I," returned Corfe, rather sneeringly. "I never smoke them."

"I beg your pardon. I was forgetting you were

a swell, and smoked nothing under a penny. I hope your cane is no worse. I saw you pottering about with it," said Delane with a smile.

"Pottering about with it! Why, if I had not scattered the paper with my stick you would not have been able to put the fire out with your feet. But you look thirsty, and I feel half stifled. Come and have a drink."

"Won't I just! Will you bear us company, Balmaine? All right; come along. I shall be back in ten minutes, Milnthorpe, and there is enough copy for the present."

CHAPTER XVI.

CORFE.

CORFE ordered absinthe. Balmaine and his colleague drank beer.

" How do you like Geneva ? " Delane asked.

Alfred said he liked it very well; and well he might. The café garden in which they sat commanded a magnificent prospect. On one side of them, far away, towered the storm-swept peaks of the Pennine Alps, on the other rose the wood-crowned heights of the purple Jura, while, almost at their feet, flowed swiftly the arrowy and amethystine Rhone, bearing on its bosom the tribute of a thousand glaciers. Hard by was a broad boulevard, fringed with trees and lined with handsome shops, the windows of most of them resplendent with gold and precious stones. People were sitting under awnings outside the cafés, sipping coffee and absorbing ices, and the streets, though sufficiently thronged to be lively, were not unpleasantly crowded. What a change from Calder ! Balmaine could hardly believe that a week had not yet elapsed since he left home. And a corresponding change

had been wrought in his spirits; never since his
father's death had he felt so free from care and so
full of hope.

"Is this your first visit to Switzerland?" asked
Corfe, as he carelessly sipped his absinthe.

"Not only that; it is my first visit to the Continent."

"You are like me, I think, not much of a
traveller," put in Delane. "I had never been on
the Continent before I landed at Calais on my way
here. I suppose you have spent half your life on
the Continent, Corfe?"

"A good deal of it, at any rate," said Corfe, com-
placently, as if to spend half one's life in foreign
countries was something to be proud of.

"Do you prefer it to England?"

"That depends on circumstances. If I had ten
thousand a year, I should probably prefer England;
but as I have a good deal less than ten thousand
shillings, I prefer the Continent. You can get far
more enjoyment out of life on a little abroad than
you can at home. I wonder poor people don't emi-
grate from England *en masse*, by gad!"

"That would be a bad job for the rich, though,"
observed Delane, "they would have neither servants nor tenants."

"Serve 'em right."

"Why, Corfe, I thought you were a Conservative!"

"If I were rich I probably should be, but being poor, I am naturally a Rad," returned Corfe, with a pleasant, almost gay laugh, which showed a set of strong white teeth. "But, really, I have been so long abroad that I have ceased to take any interest in home politics.

At this moment a white-faced little man, with little black eyes, came up, and, after making a profound salute, exchanged a few words with Corfe in Italian.

"You know Italian, then," said Balmaine, when the newcomer was gone.

"I should do," replied Corfe. "I received half my education in Italy. Yes, I think I know Italy and the Italians better than I know England and the English. And I like the life there. Geneva is all very well, but give me Florence or Milan, Naples or the Baths of Lucca."

"The Baths of Lucca?" said Balmaine. "What are they like?"

The mention of the place made him think of the lost Hardys. It was at Lucca that Philip Hardy had negotiated several of his largest drafts.

"Lucca is an awfully nice place, I can tell you. We used always to go there for the season; my father goes there still."

"How long is that ago, Mr. Corfe?"

"Why, were you ever there?"

"Have I not just said that this is my first visit

to the Continent? I take a great interest in Italy, and long intensely to see it, though."

"I almost forget how long it is since I was last at Lucca—perhaps ten years. But we used to live there part of every year. *Per Bacco!* I wish I was there now."

"If you like Italy so much, why don't you go back there?" Delane asked.

"For a very good reason; because I am under the necessity of living, though, 'pon my word, I often think it is not worth the trouble. And if life is easy in Italy, it is far from easy to make a living there. Greece is not a bad country, but it has the same fault."

"You have been in Greece, then?" said Balmaine.

"Yes; Hellas is one of the countries I have lived in. Egypt is another. I am a rolling stone, Mr. Balmaine, a fact which probably accounts for my having gathered so little moss. It is your stop-at-homes who make money."

"I must not stop here any longer, though," exclaimed Delane, rising from his seat, "or I shall make no copy. I suppose we shall have nothing from you for a few days, Balmaine?"

"Mr. Gibson said there was no hurry, that I might take a day or two before buckling to; and I must look out for lodgings. But I don't like being idle, and as Mr. Gibson has so much to do, I must do my best to help him."

"He said so, did he?" asked the sub-editor, with a significant smile. "I wish—however, you will see for yourself. As for lodgings, I think I can put you in the way of finding a pension that will suit you. Can you look in at the office about nine o'clock to-night, and I will take you to my place? Madame Guichard will find you quarters on reasonable terms."

Alfred thanked Delane for his offer, and agreed to meet him as proposed, whereupon the latter, who had outstayed his ten minutes by half-an-hour, ran back to his work.

"I live quite alone," said Corfe. "I have a room for which I pay fifteen francs a week, and I cook my own breakfast. My other meals I get at first one place, then at another. It is quite as cheap, and I don't like pensions. You have to pay for your dinner whether you eat it or not, and you get the same dishes and meet the same people every day. But you may perhaps prefer it; *chacun à son goût*, you know. If Madame Guichard asks you too much, try my plan. I know where you can get a good room for fifteen francs, perhaps less, if economy is an object with you?"

Alfred said that economy was very much an object with him. He thought it best to make no disguise on that score, but he observed that, before trying Corfe's plan, he would like to see what Madame Guichard could do for him.

" I guessed as much," went on Corfe, " economy is an object to everybody on the *Helvetic*, I think, except the swells—Leyland, Mayo and Gibson. But as for us moneyless folks, we are beggars; we are even worse—we are slaves. For what is a man, placed between the alternatives of work which he detests and starvation, but a slave ? "

" At that rate," replied Alfred with a laugh, " we are all slaves, and slavery is a condition of life. But, for my part, I see no harship in work."

" You misunderstand me. I said work which you detest. There are some sorts of work I like—writing for the *Helvetic*, for instance—though they do give me 'so little for it. But I hate giving lessons. I can make my copy when and where it pleases me ; but teaching must be done at the time appointed, whether you are in the humour or not ; and it is always the same infernal round. Pupils are so awfully stupid, too, and mine being mostly grown up, I cannot relieve my feelings by telling them so.

" Oh, I did not know you gave lessons."

" I am obliged, or you may be sure I would not. It is a case of *force majeure*, Mr. Balmaine. Won't you have another glass of beer ? No ! Well, then, if you have nothing particular to do, I will show you a few of our principal buildings and streets, so that you may know your way about."

The offer was accepted, and the two walked about for an hour or more. Corfe talking pleasantly about the countries he had visited and the people he had met. Before they separated Balmaine accepted an invitation to "take a bit of supper" with him on the following Saturday evening.

Alfred did not quite know what to make of Corfe. Gibson and Delane he liked, and felt sure that he should find in them agreeable colleagues; but Corfe was less easily read, and his cynical remarks, an occasional hardness of tone, and an indefinable something in his manner, made Balmaine suspect that he was selfish, and might be insincere. But he could be extremely pleasant when he liked, and it was possible that he might improve on further acquaintance. He was a likely man, too, having been so much in Italy, to ask about the missing Hardys. But that would come later; it was too soon yet to begin making inquiries.

CHAPTER XVII.

THE PENSION GUICHARD.

AFTER dining at his hotel—a very modest one, near the station—Balmaine strolled over the Pont du Mont Blanc to the Jardin Anglais and listened to the martial music of a band while the sun went down behind the Jura and the crescent moon rose above the Savoyard hills. The scene was lovely, the time bewitching and propitious for thought; and if it had not been for a neighbouring clock striking nine his appointment with Delane might have been forgotten.

A few minutes later he was at the office of the *Helvetic News*. He found the sub-editor all by himself reading proofs.

"All right," said Delane, when he saw Alfred, "I have just finished. Here comes the boy for the last slips. Gibson went away an hour ago. He always hooks it when he has seen a pull of his leader—sometimes before—and Milnthorpe is let off evening duty in consideration of coming so soon in the morning. He does the telegrams, you know—cribs them from the *Journal de Lacustrie*, an

ingenious arrangement which renders it unnecessary
for Leyland to subscribe to the Agence Havas."

The Pension Guichard was on the edge of a
green in the outskirts of the town—a low, old-
fashioned house, in a little old-fashioned garden,
which, for some not very obvious reason, was below
the level of the road. You had to go down to it
by steps. In the middle of the garden was a large
mulberry-tree, and the stuccoed front of the house
was covered with a trailing grape-vine. When
Balmaine returned to the Pension on the following
day, he saw that the garden stood in sore need of
weeding, and the woodwork of paint.

As Delane opened the door, their noses were
greeted with an odoriferous smell of roast meat
and onions, with a dash of garlic and old clothes.

"We are just in time for supper," said the sub-
editor.

As they take their seats in the little *salle à
manger*, half-a-dozen *pensionnaires* file into the
room. One, as Delane whispers to Balmaine, is a
Polish prince; another an Italian count; a third a
German baron. Alfred had never been in such
aristocratic company before. There are also three
ladies — one youthful and not ill-looking, one
moustached and middle-aged, one very old, with
painted cheeks, false teeth, and a most palpable
wig. The conversation was, naturally, in French,
and Balmaine had a difficulty in following it; for,

though he read it with ease, and wrote it fairly, his ear had not yet become attuned to the music of the language, and he expressed himself with difficulty. But the three men talked so loudly and incessantly that even if he could have spoken with facility he would not have found it very easy to make himself heard.

"They are a queer lot," whispered Delane; "they carry on like that every night, and sometimes make such an infernal noise that anybody outside might think they were Irishmen waking a corpse. There are two or three others, but they are out, and there are changes pretty nearly every week. It is no use telling you their names—you would forget them in five minutes; but, if you decide to come, I'll introduce you in form. It is not a first-class pension, by any means, but it is cheap and clean, and that's more than you can say of some pensions that are the reverse of cheap."

The supper, though composed of several courses, was very simple and quickly despatched. A vegetable soup, some boiled meat, which neither Delane nor Alfred could christen, and baked veal made three dishes, *spinach à la beurre* made a fourth, and for sweets they had stewed prunes. Everybody drank wine; but this, as the sub-editor informed Balmaine, was an extra, and not included in the pension price.

When the prunes appeared, and the men began

to smoke, Delane introduced Alfred to the landlady. Madame Guichard was a stalwart, rosy-
cheeked, middle-aged Vaudoise. She did nearly all
the household work with her own hands, and had
both cooked the supper and served it; that was the
reason why she could not see Alfred sooner. Delane
inquired if she could give his friend a bedroom. Perfectly; she would do anything to oblige a friend of
M. Delane. She had a pretty little chamber, over-
looking the garden, altogether at the disposition of
Monsieur. Would they give themselves the trouble
to mount on high and look at it? So up they
went, Madame leading the way, and discoursing
with much animation on the manifold advantages
offered by her pension—its salubrious situa ion,
vast garden, and its contiguity to the common.
And then its quietness for men of letters, like Monsieur Delane and his friend, could not be too highly
extolled. They might write all day long without
being disturbed by a single discordant sound. As
for the bedroom, it was simply delightful—there
was hardly such another *chambre de garçon* in all
Geneva. The bed in so charming a little alcove,
the window so nicely draped, the floor so brightly
waxed, the little secretaire, which would be so con-
venient for the writing of Monsieur. What could
one wish for better? It was a bedroom and a
workroom rolled into one.

" The room will do, though it might be bigger,"

10*

observes Balmaine ; " but how about the terms ? "

Madame, with Swiss keenness, guesses what Balmaine is saying, and smiles pleasantly.

" I will make Monsieur very favourable conditions," she says. " For the sleeping chamber, which is good enough for his Highness the Prince of Wales, and the pension of two repasts daily, the use of the salon and the enjoyment of the garden—everything comprised save wine and candles, I ask Monsieur only the insignificant sum of four francs. If Monsieur had not been introduced by M. Delane, for whom I have a perfect esteem, I should be obliged to charge five francs or, at any rate, four francs fifty."

Delane opens his eyes with astonishment.

" Four francs a day, without a second breakfast ! You forget that M. Balmaine will get his second breakfast in town. Four francs is much too much."

" But it is such a charming bedroom," pleads Madame. " It is really the best chamber in the pension, and Monsieur will have the enjoyment of the garden (it was about thirty feet square), and though nourishment is so frightfully dear, I keep a good table, as Monsieur has seen. No, M. Delane, I cannot accept Monsieur for less than four francs."

" I shall not let him pay a centime more than I pay, Madame Guichard," answers Delane resolutely, " and that is three francs fifty."

" But your chamber is *au troisième;* that makes a great difference."

" Well, give me a room on the third floor also," puts in Balmaine. " I think I would rather be a little higher up; it will be ever so much pleasanter."

" But, sirs, unfortunately I have not a chamber *au troisième* free."

" In that case Monsieur must look for lodgings elsewhere, Madame Guichard. I am very sorry, but it is impossible for him to pay so much as four francs."

" Oh, but he must not go elsewhere," exclaims Madame eagerly. " I do not like to separate friends; and though it is a great sacrifice I will make a little diminution. I will consent to take three francs fifty if Monsieur, on his part, will consent to pay a franc a week for service."

" I think that will do, Balmaine," says Delaine, " twenty two francs a week, all comprised, except wine and candles, is not bad. You will not do better, I am sure."

" All right," replies Alfred, " I agree."

" We are in accord then ? " asks the landlady with a smile of satisfaction. " It is a thing agreed."

" It is a thing agreed," answers Balmaine, and it was arranged that he should take possession of his room on the following morning.

"I don't think I should come to the office this week if I were you," said Delane as he walked with Alfred across La Plaine. "This is Thursday; on Saturday there is nothing going on, and we might make the tour of the lake. I can get a *permis*, so that it will cost us nothing but our grub. What do you say?"

"I should be delighted, and I think I might. Gibson said there was no need for me to begin work for a day or two. But then he is so busy."

"I know he is fond of saying so, but—well then, look here, I have a happy thought. He does nothing on Saturdays, of course, and likes to take it easy on Sundays. You write a leader to-morrow, and let him have the copy when he drops in during the afternoon. He will be delighted, and you will be secure in his good graces for ever."

"As you say, a happy thought, and I will try to profit by it; but what on earth must I write about? I am forbidden to touch on politics; and if I were not, my political opinions are not those of the *Helvetic News*."

"What does that matter?" said Delane, in a tone which implied that he did not quite see the relevancy of Balmaine's observation. "You can easily fake up something. If you do not look in at the office to-morrow, we shall, at any rate, meet at Madame Guichard's. Meanwhile I will get the *permis*."

As Alfred wended his way homeward, he entered into a mental calculation about ways and means.

His salary was to be seventy-five francs a week, equal
to three pounds, so, after deducting the pound he
had to send home, he would have just two to live
upon. His lodgings would cost him twenty-two
francs; as he had to provide fire and lights, and
there might be other extras, it would not be safe to
call it less than twenty-five. Dinners in town and
odds and ends would run away with at least ten
francs more, so that for clothing, travelling, and
the unforeseen, he could not reckon on more than
fifteen francs—twelve shillings and sixpence a week
—enough for his own personal wants, perhaps, and
he must cut his coat according to his cloth, but not
enough to make any long journeys in search of Vera
Hardy. Still, as he had a fairly stocked wardrobe
to start with, and three or four pounds in his pocket,
he might, by practising a rigid economy, possibly do
something, when he had got to know people better
and ascertained which way the land lay. For the
moment he could only watch and wait: later in the
season, if he could obtain a holiday, he would cross
the Helvetic Alps—if need be, on foot—and make
inquiries at every place about the Italian lakes and
in Upper Italy, which Philip Hardy's letters to his
father showed he had visited, provided he had the
wherewithal. In the meantime he would work very
hard at Italian, the study of which he had already
begun, and try to turn an honest penny by doing
something for one or other of the London papers.

CHAPTER XVIII.

LEYLAND AND MAYO.

MR. LEYLAND, the proprietor of the *Helvetic News*, was a tall, good-looking man, with a heavy moustache, dark hair—which he parted in the middle—an imposing presence and a plausible tongue. He neither wrote for the paper nor paid much attention to the details of the business, but he was great at giving orders, drawing cheques, entertaining people of distinction, and giving the *coup de grace* to hesitating advertisers ; yet he did not commit the error of making himself too common, never interfering unless "some big thing" was at stake, when his grand manner and amazing statements about the circulation of the paper were generally successful. He was equally clever at raising the wind, and on several occasions, when the paper seemed to be at the last extremity, had contrived, by some bold stroke or ingenious combination, to keep it on its legs. His latest feat of the sort was persuading the American banker mentioned by Gibson to take an interest in the paper (albeit the fact was not generally known), and grant the proprietor an almost unlimited over-draft.

Mayo, Leyland's manager and second in command, was a slightly built young fellow with sharp grey eyes, blonde complexion, and a quick, vivacious manner. He was full of fire and energy and as industrious as Leyland was the reverse, conducted all the business correspondence of the paper, looked after the accounts, and kept his eye on everything. Like his chief, he was nothing if not enterprising, and their enterprise generally took the form of spending money. If profuse outlay could ensure success, then might the *Helvetic News* count on a brilliant future.

On the day after Balmaine's first appearance in the office, Leyland and Mayo were engaged in conversation in the former's room—a handsome, luxuriously furnished apartment, one side of which was covered with a great map of Europe, the other adorned with valuable engravings.

" Has anything come in this morning ? " asks Leyland, as he leans back in his fauteuil and lazily smokes a fine Havanna cigar.

" Nothing to mention—orders for a thousand francs from Paris and eight hundred from Baden."

" Nothing from Bevis ? "

" I did not expect anything—he has only just got to work."

" Late, is he not ? "

" Very. I have been urging him to start for a month past, both by letter and telegram ; but when he once gets down to that villa of his in the Riviera he is hard to move, and whatever you say or do he always takes his own time."

"Always; but for all that he is the best canvasser we have."

"Rather. I don't know what we should do without him. I wish he was not quite so expensive, though. I have just been looking up his account, and his commission last year amounted to fifteen thousand francs, and his travelling expenses to eight."

"Nearly a thousand pounds sterling—rather stiff that. But he gets more advertisements than all the other fellows put together, so we must not complain. Where is he now?"

"At Florence. It is no use going farther south at this time of the year—hardly any use going even to Florence, I am afraid. Then by Milan and Turin to the Italian lakes, Locarno and Bellinzona, and over the Gothard to Lucerne. Then he will do the Bernese Oberland, call at Basel and Berne, and be here, I expect, in about six weeks."

"A good programme. He should do a lot of business."

"Sure to do. He always does. He has three of the best qualifications for an advertising canvasser a man can have—fine manners, ready tact, and a tongue that would almost talk a knot out of a tree, as Harman would say. I know nobody to be compared with him, except you, Leyland—if you would work."

"I'll take care I don't," answered Leyland with a laugh. "I know a trick worth two of that, Mayo. I would rather watch others work. That reminds me, though I really don't see why it should, that I had a question to ask about finance. How do we stand with Harmans?"

"Sixty thousand francs to our debit. Will they stand it do you think?"

"What a question, Mayo! They have stood it, or we shouldn't have got the money."

"Will they let it stand, I should say?"

"What else can they do? And if we want more they will let us have it; and the more we owe them the safer we are. They cannot afford to pull us up, and we cannot afford to pay them off."

"That is quite true; especially the latter," returned Mayo with an amused smile, "and I assure you I never thought of anything so absurd as paying them off. I only feared that they might possibly bother us with questions and request us to reduce the account."

"Not they; there is no reason why they should, at any rate at present; and I have got the length of Robert Harman's foot. He called last night."

"About business?"

"No; he wanted to introduce an American general and his wife to our family circle, as he put it; and we asked them all to dinner for next Monday. By the way, have you seen the new assistant editor yet? Harman was asking about him."

"Not yet. The fellow may be useful if he has anything in him."

"Of course he may, but now we have got Milnthorpe we might have done without him."

"That is true; but don't you see what a pull it gives us over Gibson? This new fellow, Balmaine, will always be ready to step into the other's shoes; and, to tell the truth, I am getting rather out of conceit with Gibson. He is lazy, his leaders are stale, and Balmaine would do the work for half his screw."

"I dare say. But you forgot that Gibson has a three years' agreement."

"No, I don't; but it is a queer agreement that one cannot get out of, and I have no doubt we shall find a way of getting out of this when the time comes. Halloa! there's a whistle, put your ear to the spout, Mayo."

"Mr. Robert Harman would be glad to see Mr. Leyland," says Mayo, still holding the tube to his ear.

The next moment the door opens and in walks the American banker. A large man all over—hair long, hat tilted back on his head, eyes all aglow with excitement, clean shaven fresh-coloured face

and an eager look, as if he had just conceived some
new idea and was burning to give it birth.

"Good day, gentlemen, good day," he exclaimed,
in a loud and hearty voice, shaking hands with both
Leyland and Mayo at the same time, "how is the
Helvetic News to-day?"

"First rate," says Leyland with his most urbane
smile. "We had several thousand francs
worth of advertisements this morning, and the
season is only just beginning. Now Bevis has got
to work we shall have as many every day."

"Glad to hear it. Nothing like going a-head,
and you do go a-head, there is no mistake about
that, we cashed drafts yesterday that make your
account more than sixty thousand on the wrong
side."

"So Mayo was saying just now," quietly
observes Leyland, "and to tell you the truth, I am
surprised it is not more. You have no idea what
the expenses of a daily paper are ; and we are only
just emerging from winter, which, as you know,
is our worst time, a great deal going out and very
little coming in. But now the tide is turning, and
in a few weeks we shall be flush. I dare say,
though, we shall have to ask you for another ten
thousand francs or so in the meantime."

"The devil you will! Well, draw it as mild as
you can, for though we want to give your
enterprise all the support in our power we are not

quite made of money, and I have partners. So far
as I am personally concerned I look on a daily
paper here as a grand fact, and the *Helvetic News*,
properly worked, is destined, I do believe to become
a great power. It will help in the realisation of
my design to make Geneva the centre of
European travel for the English-speaking people of
three continents. We are adding a large news-
room and lounge to our offices, which will be open
free to all travellers. I want to get up a company
for building a Casino; we will undertake to place
half the shares; and I mean next summer but one
—it is too late for this—to get up an international
boat-race on the lake here—-between English and
American amateur crews, of course—and in the
autumn we must have both flat races and steeple-
chases; and I am organizing a system of circular
notes and cosmopolitan credits that will place us in
communication with every respectable banking
house in the civilized world. We must spare no
effort to attract attention to the place, and make it
so fashionable and attractive that no traveller can
feel that he has done the continent at all unless he has
spent a few days at Geneva. It is a big enterprise,
I know, but I am determined to carry it through,
and I attach great importance to your co-operation
and the influence of the *Helvetic News*."

All this was said with great energy and rapidity,
and almost in a breath.

"We will do all we can, you may be sure of that," Leyland answered warmly, "your interest is our interest, more travellers mean more money-changing for you, more subscribers and more advertisements for us. You may count on our hearty co-operation in all these schemes you have been mentioning, Harman. The paper is always at your disposal for paragraphs and articles—anything you like, in fact. But then you must not talk of stopping the tap, you know."

"I was not talking of stopping the tap. I was only asking you to draw it mild, and be as moderate as you can. I am quite satisfied; but our New York and London houses may not see matters in precisely the same light, remember."

"Halloa! the whistle again; what is it, Mayo?"

"Mr. Gibson and Mr. Balmaine would like to know when they can see Mr. Leyland and Mr. Mayo."

"Say we are engaged, and tell them to come in an hour."

"Let them come in now," interposed the banker. "I have very little more to say, and I want to speak to Gibson and make the acquaintance of his new assistant."

So the newcomers were ushered into the room and Balmaine was introduced in due form to the assembled trio, who gave him a gracious reception, though Leyland's manner was marked by a certain condescension, as if to signify to Alfred that the proprietor of a newspaper was something very different from its assistant editor."

"I am glad to make your acquaintance, Mr. Balmaine," said the banker warmly. "I hope we shall be good friends, and if you will let me, I may sometimes profit by your literary skill. I have bothered Mr. Gibson occasionally, but now, when I want an article put into shape, I shall come to you. An editor-in-chief ought to write very little. His business is to supervise others, revise what they write and furnish them with ideas. Is not that so, Gibson?"

"It is exactly what I have been saying ever since I came here; and I have no doubt that with Mr. Balmaine's help I shall be able to give more time to the general supervision of the paper; and I hope we shall succeed in making it even brighter and better than, as everybody admits, it is at present."

"That is hardly possible, I think, Gibson," said Harman, the suspicion of a smile playing about the corners of his mouth. "Considering the means at your disposal, the *Helvetic News* is admirably edited. And now I want all of you to lunch with me—second breakfast they call it here—at my hotel on Sunday. I mean the entire editorial staff, and Mr. Leyland and Mr. Mayo. Can that be managed, Gibson? I mean with reference to the duties of the paper, for you unfortunates have to work on Sundays."

Gibson declared that it could be managed very easily, and accepted the invitation on behalf of Delane and Milnthorpe. Alfred accepted it on his own, and it was accepted as a matter of course by the manager and proprietor.

" I like your Mr. Balmaine," said Harman, when the former and Gibson had taken their leave, " he has a good face, and is of better breeding, I should say, than either the chief or his subs."

" Yes, he seems a likely sort of chap ; I dare say he will do," answered Leyland carelessly. "I say, Harman, it's awfully good of you to invite those fellows to breakfast."

" Not at all. I honour writers of every class, and like to stand well with them."

" That is all very well; but I cannot say that I honour newspaper writers much—I know too much about them. They have no principles; they write anything you tell them. Take Balmaine now; I know absolutely nothing of him, but I would bet my bottom dollar that I could make him write a Tory leader one day and a Radical leader the next."

" I don't believe you could, Leyland ; he is not a man of that sort, and I would back my opinion with a bet if there were any way of bringing it to a test."

" Which at present there is not," said Leyland
half jestingly, " unless we become Conservative."

" Which you won't," returned Harman, who did
not seem to appreciate the joke, " unless you want to
forfeit my support."

" That settles the matter," laughed Leyland, " for
we don't want to forfeit your support; anything but
that.　And we will assume, if you like, that Balmaine
is that phenomenal being, a journalist with principles."

" You may say what you like about him," said
the banker, who appeared just a little huffed by the
other's chaff; " I have taken a fancy to that young
man, and, if he can write a smart letter, I will try
to throw something in his way."

" Those are the three men who control the destinies
of the *Helvetic News*, and, to a certain extent, our
destinies," said Gibson to Alfred, when they were
outside ; " what do you think of them ? "

" I will tell you when I know them better," was
Alfred's cautious answer ; " you cannot learn much
of people's character in a casual interview of a few
minutes.　What do you think of them, Mr. Gibson ?
You have had far more opportunities of judging
them than I have."

" That is quite true.　Well, I will tell you my
opinion when you have had an opportunity of form-
ing yours."

Balmaine had called at the office a few minute

previously to ask if he would be wanted before Sunday. Gibson replied in the negative, and, as we have seen, took him below to pay his respects to the proprietor and manager. As they passed through the spacious and well appointed offices, Alfred noticed with some surprise how large was the staff of clerks, all of whom seemed to be fully occupied; but the most prominent object was a huge thief-proof, fire-resisting safe that could hardly fail to impress casual visitors, paper merchants, type founders, and others with a sense of the importance of the *Helvetic News*, and of the vastness of the cash and other securities that needed so much safe-guarding.

CHAPTER XIX.

ON THE LAKE.

In after years a great many things both grave and gay befell Balmaine; but the impression of his first sail round the lake remained ever green in his memory. The day was perfect, the early morning air fresh and elastic, the scene about the port striking and animated. The shore lined with fresh-leaved trees and handsome buildings, the quaint houses of the old town, climbing up the heights crowned by the grey towers of St. Peter and the golden cupolas of the Russian Church—all was new to him; and although the picturesque never palls on the lover of nature, the sense of novelty and the gratification of long-cherished desires add piquancy to enjoyment. The reality, too, exceeded his expectation. The hour being early the Alps were not yet visible, and on the rugged sides of the Jura were reposing masses of cloud so white, so still, and in form so fantastic and weird, that they might have been vast snow-fields, icy crags, and tremendous glaciers, blocking up the horizon and reaching high as heaven. Yet, still as they seem, the clouds move.

They creep slowly up the gullies and roll back from
the pine forests, and then, between the white mass
and the dark back-ground, mountain and forest show
a tint of blue so deep and tender that it might
be one of heaven's own windows, or the way into
fairyland. Now to the south the morning glory is
retreating before the advancing day, and the dia-
demed peaks of the Pennine Alps, emerging from a
silvery sea, stand revealed in all their beauty and fill
the sky with their majestic presence. A few minutes
later and all the vast stretch of country, from the
mountains of Savoy to the Dent du Midi, from the
snows of Mont Blanc to the gorges of Mont Reculet,
is bathed in brilliant sunlight, and the crystal waters
of the lake sparkle like liquid diamonds in a setting
of azure.

The region round about is, moreover, rich in
historic associations. Westward, the Fort de l'Ecluse
guards the famous pass, cleft un-numbered years ago
by the great Rhone glacier, and through which, by
comparison only the other day, the greatest of the
Cæsars followed on the traces of the flying Helvetians.
Atilla and his Huns wasted the land with fire and
sword, Teutonic tribes marched along the shores of
the lake to the sack of Rome, and the valley once
echoed to the tread of Napoleon's legions as they
marched to the conquest of Italy. Yet, charmed
with the beauty of the landscape as Balmaine un-
doubtedly was, and delighted as he might be with

the clearness of the sky and the serenity of the weather, I would not aver that all these reflections were suggested to his mind or that he gave much heed to the historic associations of the scene before him. For he had more companions than he counted on, and was too much disturbed with questions and exclamations to give himself up to thoughts of the sublime or contemplation of the beautiful.

In the Pension Guichard, as the reader is already aware, were three lady lodgers, each of whom, as Alfred, when he took up his quarters there, speedily learnt, bore the name of Von Schmidt and represented a distinct generation of that ancient and respectable family. There were Madame von Schmidt, the grandmother; Madame Karl von Schmidt, the mother; and Mademoiselle von Schmidt, the daughter. Being Germans, they naturally all played on the piano. Madame von Schmidt had been a teacher of music, Madame Karl was a teacher of music, and Mademoiselle, a pretty little blonde of seventeen, was learning to be a teacher of music. Except early in the morning, before the other lodgers went out, and in the evening when they had come in, Madame Guichard's piano was seldom silent, for when Madame Karl was not giving lessons her daughter was generally practising with preternatural energy. A distracted neighbour, who stayed at home all day long and was writing a book, had threatened Madame Guichard with an action ; but Switzerland being a free country, she defied him, and bade the Von Schmidts, with whom she was very intimate, to play on.

On the Friday evening Delane told Alfred, in a sheepish sort of way, that he had invited Madame Karl and her daughter to go with them round the lake.

"It will not cost us anything," he said. "I have got free tickets for all."

This announcement did not seem very greatly to delight Balmaine. He foresaw that he should have to escort and entertain the elder lady, who happened to have a very decided moustache, a very loud voice, and rolled in her walk like a sailor, while Mademoiselle would fall to the lot of the sub-editor.

"They are very nice," urged Delane deprecatingly, "and not too rich, and have to work hard all day long. The trip will be a great pleasure for them and do Mademoiselle a power of good ; she is looking very pale, as you may have noticed."

It was impossible to resist the young fellow's appeal. "By all means let them come," Alfred said, "and we will do our best to make the trip pleasant for them."

It was pleasant for all. Madame and Mademoiselle were in ecstasies of delight, and Alfred found the elder lady a much more agreeable com-

panion than he had expected. Despite her
moustache and ungainly walk, she was a highly
cultivated woman, and had a frank matronly
manner, which at once engaged Balmaine's liking,
and her story won his respect. He had already
heard something of it from Madame Guichard
and Delane. Her husband, much older than she,
was an Austrian officer of high rank, who had died
a few years previously at Vienna very much in debt,
owing to some unfortunate speculations in which he
had embarked. All that he possessed did not suffice
to discharge his liabilities, and Madame Karl found
herself utterly destitute, with her old mother and
a young daughter absolutely dependent on her. A
brilliant pianist, she might possibly have earned
a livelihood in the Austrian capital by giving
lessons, but the humiliation was greater than she
could bear, and, having a few friends at Geneva,
she went thither and set up us a teacher of music.
Her undoubted ability soon brought her some good
paying pupils, and she was earning an income that
would have made them very comfortable had she
not thought it her duty to pay off her husband's
debts. All that remained, after providing for their
modest wants, was, every quarter, remitted to his
creditors at Vienna.

"As I helped my poor husband to spend his
money," she said, "it is only right that I should
help to pay his debts."

And then she spoke of her life in Austria, Milan, and other places.

"So you have not only visited Italy, but lived there?" asked Alfred.

"Certainly. During the occupation we lived in Northern Italy many years. Ida, my daughter, was born at Venice."

It struck Balmaine that Madame Karl could, perchance, give him some information about the Hardys. She was evidently a woman whom he might trust, and he proceeded to give her an outline of the case, without, however, saying anything very definite about the fortune. It was not necessary that he should, and both Warton and Artful had warned him that to make much noise about it would almost certainly bring forth false claimants.

Madame Karl listened to the tale with great interest. "I wish I could help you," she said; "but I don't think I ever heard of this man; at any rate, under the name of Hardy. It is not likely that I should. I was on the other side, you know."

"If he was taken prisoner or executed, I thought you might possibly have heard some mention of him."

"It is not likely, there were so many of them; and if I did, I have forgotten. If we had not been turned out of Italy, I have no doubt I could find out whether he was taken by the Austrians. You may, however, be sure of one thing—he is not in

prison now. Why should our Government care to
keep Italian prisoners after we left the country?
They were all released."

"That is a new light," answered Alfred musingly.
"I never thought of that before; it knocks Mr. Artful's theory on the head. Well, if Philip Hardy is
not in prison where can he be?"

"Dead, I should say," returned Madame Karl
promptly; "conspirators and soldiers of fortune
have short lives, and your Monsieur Hardy appears
to have been both. But why don't you ask Colonel
Bevis? If anybody can tell you he can."

"Who is Colonel Bevis?"

"Why, don't you know? It is he who keeps
the *Helvetic News* going—the best advertisement
canvasser, they say, on the Continent. He has
served in the British army, I think. At any rate,
he was one of Garibaldi's men, and deeply impli-
cated in every revolutionary movement in Northern
Italy."

"How did he come to be an advertisement canvasser?"

"By being poor, I suppose. Men like him
generally are poor. We cannot always choose our
destinies, or I should not be a music mistress.
He is very fortunate in having secured such a
position. M. Delane says that he makes very
much money, and he spends his winters in the
Riviera and in Italy, and his summers in Switzer-

land and South Germany. It is, perhaps, not so fine a thing to be a canvasser as to command a regiment, but I am sure Colonel Bevis is better off now than when he was organizing secret societies in Lombardy and Venice, or fighting with the Red Shirts in Naples. He is the man for you ; he knows Italy well. So does M. Corfe ; but I would rather speak to the Colonel if I were you."

" I am much obliged to you for suggesting the idea, Madame von Schmidt, and I shall certainly profit by it ; but you do not tell me where I shall find this remarkable colonel-canvasser. Is he in Geneva ? "

" Not at all; he is probably on a journey. I dare say M. Delane will tell us."

Delane, who was promenading round the deck with Ida, being called, informed them that Colonel Bevis was travelling, and would no doubt, in accordance with his usual custom, be at Geneva some time during the summer.

And then the subject dropped, and Balmaine occupied himself with contemplating the scenery, while Delane and Ida resumed their walk round the deck.

" Journalism is a very honourable profession, M. Balmaine," observed Madame Karl, apropos of nothing in particular.

" Unquestionably," answered Alfred.

" But not a very profitable one, I fear."

"I beg your pardon, Madame Karl, for some people it is very profitable."

"Ah, yes, but not for such people as you and our friend, M. Delane."

"Not at present, perhaps; but there is no telling what the future has in store for us, and Delane is a very clever young fellow, I think."

"The future! No, as you say, there is no telling what the future has in store for us. You think it has something good—young people always do—but those who are verging on fifty know that it must have some evil, and may have much. Make the most of your youth, M. Balmaine; it will not last too long. Do you know I am rather anxious about Ida?"

"Why? She looks very well."

And so she did, for though she was rather *petite* and her face somewhat too broad, Ida, with her flaxen hair, dreamy blue eyes, cream white neck and pink cheeks did not come very far short of being an ideal Teutonic beauty.

"She looks very well," repeated Alfred.

"Yes, the child is pretty, is she not?" said the mother, proudly, "but she is excited and flushed now. Poor girl, I can neither give her a *dot* nor leave her a fortune, so she must work—perhaps I make her work too hard. But she is very clever and ardent, and besides singing and the piano she learns the modern languages, so she is sure to get her living, don't you think so, M. Balmaine ? "

" Very sure, I should say; and with that face of hers, and so many accomplishments, she is sure to get a husband."

" So much more reason why she should learn to make money, M. Balmaine," returned Madame Karl, with rather a bitter laugh, " she may have to keep her husband—some women have—or to pay his debts. I was a music mistress's daughter, and teaching music myself, when General von Schmidt—he was captain then—became my husband. It was a love match, though to look at me now you wouldn't think so. But what would have become of us if I had not been able to turn an honest penny ? "

Alfred inferred from this conversation, and even more from Madame Karl's manner, that she had some fear that Delane and her daughter might become too fond of each other. The vigilance with which she watched them was amusing; she seldom let them go beyond earshot, never out of sight.

CHAPTER XX.

HARMAN'S BREAKFAST.

CORFE'S supper was a decided success; none the less so, perhaps, owing to its somewhat Bohemian character, for his rooms were on the third floor of a ramshackle shabby-looking house, in an unfashionable quarter, and his guests were far from belonging to the *crême de la crême* of Genevan society. They were very merry fellows, however, and one of them, whom from his long dishevelled hair and generally harum-scarum appearance Alfred took to be an artist, kept the table in a roar. Corfe did the part of host to perfection, sang a good song to his own accompaniment on a guitar, told some excellent stories, and his manner was as genial and agreeable as it had been unpleasant and repelling on the day Balmaine first met him. He seemed to be quite another man, yet the hard lines about the mouth, and a fleeting frown that once or twice overshadowed his face, showed that he had it in him to be as cynical and ill-humoured as he was now amiable and good-tempered.

"What do you think of Corfe?" asked Alfred of Delane, as they walked home together across the plain. "He rather puzzles me."

"He puzzles everybody, I think. He was very nice to-night, wasn't he? He has two quite opposite humours, and you have seen him now in both. I sometimes think that he is one of those fellows who have missed their tip somehow, and come down in life. And that's what Gibson says, and Gibson is uncommonly shrewd. He says if ever he saw a disappointed, discontented man, that man is Corfe. All the same, some people like him and speak well of him, and in spite of his ill-temper and that, I fancy he is a very good fellow at bottom. Only he is very ready to take offence, and when he falls out with anybody he lets 'em have it hot."

"You think he is a sort of man that one ought to keep on good terms with, then?"

"I am sure."

"Well, then, I will try to keep on good terms with him, and if he continues to be half as amiable as he showed himself to-night I shall have no difficulty."

Harman's breakfast was not nearly so pleasant as Corfe's supper. The wines were exquisite and the viands everything that could be desired; but the meal was intolerably long, and as the banker, Leyland, Mayo, and Gibson kept the conversation

pretty much to themselves, and Delane and Milnthorpe, awed by the presence of their superiors,
never opened their mouths, except to eat and drink,
Balmaine did not find it very lively, and felt it
a decided relief when the senior sub-editor, speaking for the first time, suggested that it was about
time they went to the office.

"Indeed it is," said Gibson in a rather thick
voice, for he had taken very kindly to his wine;
" why it is actually after three o'clock. I must go
too and get my leader done. I shall be over in
a few minutes, Delane. I will just stay and finish
this cigar."

" If you think this suitable," observed Alfred in
an undertone, drawing some " copy " from his
pocket, "it may perhaps save you the trouble of
writing a leader. It is an article on the Eastern
Question."

"Thank you very much," returned the editor
with a gratified smile; "will you let me cast my
eye over it for a moment ? "

"It will do very well, Mr. Balmaine" (turning
over the leaves); "just the thing we want—crisp,
lively, and not too long. You can let Lud have
it. But you need not go just yet. If Lud gets
the copy in an hour it will be quite time
enough."

"Yes, stay a few minutes longer," put in Harman, who had overheard the conversation, " and

won't you take another cigar? I have something
to say to you."

Thus pressed Alfred took another cigar and resumed his seat, and the banker, after a few in-
different remarks, asked him if he would like to
write some letters for an American paper. Alfred
said he should very much like to write some
letters for an American paper.

"I thought so," said the banker. "Well, you
call at my office to-morrow about eleven and I
will introduce you to the editor of a paper at
Pitsburg, who, I think, on my recommendation,
will be glad to make an arrangement with you."

Balmaine replied that nothing would give him
greater pleasure, and shortly afterwards he took
his leave and betook himself to the office of the
Helvetic News.

During the week that followed Alfred got fairly
into harness, and for some time afterwards his
life, so far as appeared, was regular and uneventful. So far as appeared, because, as a matter of
fact, no life can be really uneventful. Every day
brings its incidents, and, though we know it not,
any one of them, even the most commonplace, may
be big with fate. What, for instance, can be more
ordinary than going to bed and getting up, admiring a landscape or watching a sunset? yet we must
all, sooner or later, go to bed and get up for the last
time, and take our last view of earth and sky. A

casual introduction to a stranger may lead to moment-
ous consequences, and a chance meeting in a railway
carriage form a turning point in a man's destiny.

But though Balmaine settled down to steady
work, and the days went on unmarked by any
startling event, his life at Geneva was decidedly
interesting. If there had been nothing else he
would have found amusing occupation for his leisure
in studying the characters of the people he met,
and watching the little intrigues and comedies that
were always going on about him. At the office
there was jealousy between uptsairs and down, for
the clerks were allowed to canvass for advertisements, and paid a commission of twenty-five per
cent. on all they obtained; the sub-editors were not,
and this was a sore grievance with Milnthorpe and
Delane. Gibson was both able and shrewd; but,
as Alfred soon found out, he liked to take things
very easy, and make-believe that he worked very
hard. Delane, who was full of energy, did more
real work in a day than the chief did in a week.
"He did not do much before you came," the sub
one day observed to Balmaine, "now he does next
to nothing."

This was quite true. There were at least three
days a week on which Gibson did not write a line
for the paper—did nothing, in fact, but answer a
few letters and look over a few proofs.

"Between ourselves," went on Delane, "I don't

think it was very 'cute of him to let you come at
all; there really isn't work for more than three, and
being by far the best paid of the lot, if there should
be a change, he is the most likely to have to go.
At any rate I should think so."

" How much has he ? "

" Three hundred and fifty francs a week."

" Fourteen pounds."

" Yes; nearly twice as much as you, me, and
Milnthorpe get, all put together. Isn't it a shame?
I have no respect either for Leyland or Mayo: they
are unmitigated ruffians, both of them."

" If they are such a bad lot why don't you leave
them ? " asked Alfred, who began to think that he
had got into rather queer company.

" Because I don't want to. The private character
of the men and their management of the paper are
nothing to me. I do my duty, and that is really all
I have to care about; and then Geneva is an uncommonly nice place. I like the life here; and
there are other reasons."

At this point the young fellow blushed a little,
and Balmaine thought of Ida von Schmidt; so, by
way of changing the subject, he made an inquiry
touching the circulation of the *Helvetic News*.

" You asked me that once before, I think," said
Delane dryly.

" So I did, and got no answer," said Alfred,
smiling. " Is it a mystery ? "

12*

"Very much so. To be frank, I don't know what it is, and don't want to know."

"Why?"

"So that I may be under no temptation to tell lies. That is what old Bevis does."

"Does he tell lies then?"

"He does not profess to do. I mean he does not know and won't be told anything about the circulation. When anybody asks him he says, in his loftiest manner: 'That is not in my department, my dear sir, and the circulation varies so much, according to the season, that I should not like to risk telling an untruth by going into details; but I can assure you with the utmost confidence that it is large and influential.' He calls that diplomacy."

"And there are people," said Alfred, "who say there is very little difference between diplomacy and artistic lying."

He made no further inquiry about the circulation of the paper.

Milnthorpe was rather an enigma. He did his work, chiefly translating, slowly, but well, had very little to say, seemed depressed, and nobody knew where he lived. Delane thought he did not like to expose his poverty by associating with his equals, for he could not be persuaded to enter a café, and never smoked unless somebody gave him a cigar.

In addition to his office work, which he did not

find very arduous, Alfred worked at home. He
wrote a series of letters for the American editor—to
whom Harman so kindly introduced him, a certain
Dr. Pilgrim, a tall, spare man, with a white choker,
a soft voice, and an unctuous manner—of the
Pitsburg Patriot. The *Patriot*, as the doctor
informed him, was a semi-religious, high-toned,
first-class paper, circulating among first-class families. He wanted some articles on the graver aspects
of Swiss life, on the religious views of the people,
the character of their Protestantism, and, above all,
on the Old Catholic movement. At the same time
the letters, though weighty with facts, were to be
lively in style. For as the doctor rightly observed,
if newspaper articles be not readable they are of
very little use, and to be readable they must be
lively. When he asked Alfred if he thought he
could write him a few such letters as those he had
described, say four or five, the young fellow modestly
replied that he thought he could, and would do his
best. As for remuneration, the editor of this serious,
semi-religious paper remarked, with one of his
sweetest smiles, that first-class journals like the
Patriot paid twenty dollars an article irrespective
of length, "which we don't want, for everybody
knows that it is easier to pad out than to boil
down."

After thanking Dr. Pilgrim "very much," Balmaine went home rejoicing, and feeling almost as

if he had a hundred dollars (five letters at twenty
a-piece) in his pocket. He gave several days to
reading up the subjects suggested and making
inquiries, and a fortnight afterwards forwarded his
first letter to the high-toned *Patriot*. Nor did his
good fortune end here. No American journalist could
possibly pass through Geneva without calling at the
editorial offices of the *News*, to look over the files
and have a talk with the staff. Some of these
gentlemen made themselves very much at home,
and seemed to consider the sub-editors' room a
public lounge and their waste-paper baskets public
spittoons. Others were very nice fellows indeed,
and one of them, the representative of a Boston
daily, Sunday, and bi-weekly, invited Alfred (one of
whose articles in the *Helvetic* had attracted his
attention) to contribute an occasional letter " on
any darned subject he liked," and assured him that
he wrote well enough for the London *Times*, " or
any other sanguinary paper."

With these two strings to his bow Alfred came to
the conclusion that it was not necessary to make
any offerings to English papers for the present;
they might be refused; it would be better to send
his communications where they were sure of acceptance. The reception of his first letter by the *Pitsburg Patriot* was gratifying in the extreme. The
acting editor (Dr. Pilgrim not having yet reached
home) bespoke for it the particular attention of his

readers, described the writer as one of the most rising and successful of the younger generation of English journalists, and promised them further effusions from the same brilliant pen. Alfred sent a copy of the paper to Cora, whom it greatly delighted ; it was, moreover, seen by many people at Calder, and made the subject of a few complimentary remarks in the *Mercury*.

Another agreeable incident was the receipt of a letter from Artful and Higginbottom, inquiring if he still thought he should be able "to find a clue to the mystery that enveloped the fate of the unfortunate Mr. Philip Hardy and his daughter," and offering, on the part of the trustees, " to defray any reasonable charge to which he might be put in prosecuting the investigation which he had so kindly promised to make." This meant that they would pay his travelling expenses, so he should now be able, when he got a holiday, to make the journey across the Alps from which he hoped so much.

Everything seemed propitious, and the rupture of his engagement with Lizzie Hardy, which took place about this time, left him almost without a care. Although the affair had once caused him so much concern, he could now hardly think of it without laughing at his simplicity in attributing to a foolish flirtation the character of a solemn betrothal. Shortly after his arrival at Geneva he received from his sweetheart a long letter, to which he replied in due course, but not being able to make passionate protestations of love he contented himself with descriptions of the country and the people, and of his own doings and experiences. To this, rather to his satisfaction, there came no answer; and then there ensued a long silence which Alfred, whose too tender conscience began to suggest that he was treating the girl badly, was the first to break by a second letter in the style of the first. Lizzie replied in a missive which she meant to be freezing and dignified, but which (after his first surprise) Balmaine found intensely amusing. She could not imagine, she said, what induced him to write to her in the way he had done. It had never occurred to her to consider the innocent familiarities which at one time she had allowed him as implying an engagement, even if their relative positions had not rendered such a thing impossible, and she desired that the correspondence might cease with the present communication.

"Innocent familiarities! our relative positions! by Jove, that's good," soliloquised Balmaine, and though he was glad to be set free, it was some alloy to his satisfaction to think that Saintly Sam's daughter had so completely befooled him.

CHAPTER XXI.

COLONEL BEVIS.

So soon as Balmaine had got fairly into harness
Gibson took his holiday. He had worked so hard
during the previous twelvemonth, he said, that a
period of relaxation was absolutely necessary for his
health. Before going away he gave precise instructions about the editing of the paper. All the
leaders were to be written by Alfred, and none were
to touch on English politics. With this exception,
he was to have full scope. "And if you are ever
pressed for time or do not see your way to a subject,"
added the chief, "you can always get one of the
least read of English or American papers. The
Saturday Sentinel, for instance, is a capital paper to
quarry from. Its sub-leaders are often very good,
and there are always one or two that by running
through with a wet pen you can make to look as if
they were written purposely for the *Helvetic*."

Alfred modestly replied that he thought he would
rather trust to his own unaided resources; and when
Gibson returned from his holiday-making, he congratu-
lated the young fellow handsomely on the diligence

and ability with which he had discharged his duties. Another success scored by Alfred was the reproduction of one of his articles by a London paper. Delane said this was a feather in his cap. Mayo came specially into the editor's-room to inquire by whom it had been written, and said a few gracious words to Balmaine on the occasion ; for incidents like this were not alone flattering to the *amour propre* of all connected with the *Helvetic News,* they made the paper more widely known, and so helped canvassers in their quest for advertisements.

On entering the sub-editors' room one morning, Alfred was informed that Mr. Mayo wanted to see him downstairs. In the manager's room was a fine soldierly looking man, whose age might be from forty-four to fifty, but by reason of the uprightness of his carriage, the freshness of his complexion, and the lightness of his hair and moustache as yet unfrosted with white, he looked younger than his years. He was dressed with great neatness, wore the badge of some military order, and, as Balmaine subsequently heard, had a right to call himself "Chevalier."

This gentleman was Colonel Bevis, and Mayo, after introducing them to each other, mentioned that the Colonel wanted a special article written, and asked Alfred to take his instructions and put it into shape for the printer.

" It is about Rothenkirschen, Mr. Balmaine," said

the Colonel very graciously, "the new place in the Oberland, you know. They have found some dirty water, built a Kursaal and several hotels, and want to attract English and American visitors. I have taken a very good advertisement from them on condition that we reciprocate by doing a little *reclâme*, and give a special article about the place. And I can personally testify that it is most charmingly situated—on that score you can hardly exaggerate—and several highly respectable doctors are ready to take oath that the mineral waters are good for every ill that flesh is heir to. You will find all the facts in this newspaper cutting—you read German, of course—and a few observations of my own in this paper. Do you think you can shape these materials into a readable article? I shall be very much obliged if you can, because I promised the people, you know."

Alfred answered that he would do his best, and asked the Colonel if he would like to see a proof of the article in order to make sure that it was quite to his mind. The Colonel said, "Very much," and asked Alfred to be good enough to send the proof to him at the Hotel de la Grande Bretagne, where he should be visible at five P.M.

It was the first time Balmaine had done any puffing, and he hoped the description of Rothenkirschen, given in the German paper, was true, for in that case the earthly paradise was only about a

hundred miles from Geneva. The magnificent
scenery, the fine climate, and the mountain air
alone made the place worth a visit, while the charming grounds of the Kursaal, morning music, daily
excursions, evening concerts, and congenial society
rendered life in that favoured spot beyond expression delightful, and by drinking plentifully of the
waters you might live for ever and never be ill.
Alfred did not say quite all this, neither did he set
forth all the maladies for which a sojourn at
Rothenkirschen was recommended as a specific;
nevertheless he produced a really brilliant article,
and one that could hardly fail to prove satisfactory
to all concerned. As he wanted to cultivate Bevis's
acquaintance he took the proof to him instead of
sending it.

"Thank you very much, Mr. Balmaine," said the
Colonel, whom he found smoking a cigarette in the
corridor of the Bretagne; "it is very kind of you
to take so much trouble, and you add to the favour
by being so prompt. Promptitude in the eyes of an
old soldier is a high quality. This will do very
well—very well indeed:—' In the whole of Switzerland there is no spot on which nature has showered
so many blessings as the valley and village of Rothenkirschen. Whilst its great altitude insures the
purity of its invigorating air, the huge mass of
mountains to the north and east shelters it from
every inclement wind, and renders the climate as

balmy and enjoyable as that of the land in which it seemed always afternoon. The thermal establishment is begirt with fragrant fir-trees, and the gleaming glacier-born river, which rushes in tumultuous route past its walls, flows between fair gardens and green meadows into the Kirschen lake, a mile farther on.' Really, Mr. Balmaine, nothing could be better. I do not see how anybody can help going to Rothenkirschen after reading this description, and, better still, it will be sure to bring us another advertisement. There is only one thing wanting."

"And that is—"

"The name of the resident physician, Dr. Schlachtermann. Don't you think you could bring it in somehow? It would please him immensely, and make the advertisement quite sure; and he is really a clever fellow. He gave me a prescription that has quite cured my sciatica—'pon my word he did."

"How would this do?" said Alfred, taking out his pencil. "Put it in after 'patients,' you know. The sentence will now read thus: 'The invaluable qualities of the mineral waters have been proved, as well by chemical analysis as by the testimony of hundreds of patients, who, under the skilful treatment of Dr. Schlachtermann, one of the most eminent of Swiss bath physicians, have recovered health and strength, even when recovery had been deemed hopeless,' &c., &c."

"Just the thing, Mr. Balmaine, just the thing You understand exactly what I want. A few articles like that will increase our advertisements by twenty thousand francs. I have often suggested to Mayo that he should have somebody on the staff with a knowledge of German, and able to write an attractive article. Your help will be invaluable. I shall have to apply to you again. Will that appear to-morrow?"

"Certainly," said Alfred, putting the proof in his pocket, and making as if he meant to go.

"Must you go already?" said the Colonel, taking his hand. "I know you are a busy man, but if you can stay and have dinner with me I shall be very glad. It will be ready in half an hour, and 1 will release you as soon afterwards as you like."

Alfred accepted the invitation; it was what he wanted, and he did not find it difficult to lead the conversation to the subject of the Colonel's adventurous life, on which he was as loquacious as veterans are wont to be, yet at the same time very entertaining.

CHAPTER XXII.

BALMAINE LEARNS SOMETHING.

COLONEL BEVIS related his reminiscences at great length, but after he had run on for some time Balmaine took advantage of a pause to inquire how he had become connected with the Italian revolutionary movement.

"Easily enough," was the answer; "after the Crimean war was over, I wanted something to do, chance took me to Italy, and there I became acquainted with the chiefs of the party. They employed me in various capacities. I took service with Garibaldi, and fought through the campaign of 1860."

"You were one of the famous thousand of Marsala, then?"

"Yes," said the Colonel drily, lighting another cigarette. "I was one of the thousand of Marsala; the Chief made me a Colonel, and on one occasion I commanded a brigade."

"You mean Garibaldi; what a fine fellow he is!" exclaimed Balmaine enthusiastically. "And you were really a friend of his, Colonel?"

"I had that honour," replied the Colonel, rather

coolly, "and I think I was more friendly to him than he was to me."

"Do you mean that he did not treat you well? no, that is impossible."

"I do mean it. But for me he would have lost one of the most important battles of the campaign. I landed at Naples in command of reinforcements from Sicily. My instructions were to hasten to the front as quickly as possible, an engagement being momentarily expected. But we were short of supplies, and quite without money. My men wanted shoes, bread, and powder. To requisition the inhabitants would have been the worst possible policy; it might have turned them against us. What was I to do? I had, fortunately, the reputation of being a rich Englishman, so I ordered what I wanted, paid for it in drafts on my London bankers, and reached the front just in time to turn the tide of battle. If we had been only an hour later it might have gone ill with the cause, for the Chief was over-matched and hard pressed."

"And were the drafts paid?"

"Ultimately they were, of course, but if we had not won they would not have been. What I complain of Garibaldi for is that he did so little for his followers. He told the King that he wanted nothing for himself, yet he might easily have stipulated something for us—either moderate pensions or positions in the Italian army. As it was, we were just

turned adrift with next to nothing. I fought in
every battle, and was twice wounded, yet all they
gave me was the Order of the Iron Crown and
about five pounds a year! And here I am, an old
soldier, one of the thousand of Marsala, drumming
for advertisements."

"And you drum as well as you fight, I believe,
Colonel Bevis. People say you are the best canvasser
in Europe, which, after all, is something to be proud
of. You must have met a great many people in your
wanderings—did you ever meet in Italy, or elsewhere, an Englishman of the name of Hardy?"

"Hardy, Hardy!" said the Colonel thoughtfully.
"As you say, I have met very many people in my
life, so many, that a name may easily slip my
memory. Still, my memory is very good. Hardy,
Hardy! Do you mean Philip Hardy?"

"Yes, I mean Philip Hardy!" answered Balmaine eagerly; he felt as if he were on the track of
a discovery.

"Did you know him?"

"No, but I am very anxious to find out something
about him, and if you can help me I shall feel
greatly obliged!"

"He was engaged in the revolutionary movement,
wasn't he?"

"Yes, and disappeared about ten years ago!"

"Did he?" said Bevis absently. "Yes, I knew
Philip Hardy; and, though I did not meet him

often, I liked him well. He married an Italian wife and had a little girl, I think ! "

" That is just the man ! " exclaimed Alfred excitedly.

" But he did not always go under the name of Hardy. He had reasons, reasons of state let us say, for taking an alias occasionally. Is that another characteristic ? "

" It is, it is. The Philip Hardy you know is the Philip Hardy I want to find, or, at any rate, a clue to his fate ! "

" Is he a relative of yours, Mr. Balmaine ? "

" No, he has few relations, I think ; but a friend of mine, at Calder, is very anxious to find out what has become of him, and I was asked by some people in London to make inquiries. They want to have proof of his death—if he be dead ! "

" Property, I suppose ? "

" Yes, there is some property. And I have heard so much about the case, that I would like, as a matter of personal feeling, and for the gratification of a legitimate curiosity, to discover a clue to the mystery ! "

" I think I understand. But what about the little girl ? I remember seeing her at Pallanza, and a pretty little thing she was."

" She has disappeared too ! "

" By disappearing, you mean that nothing has been heard of her ? "

" Exactly ; nothing has been heard of her since old Mr. Hardy's death, ten years ago ! "

" And for more than that time Philip Hardy has been out of my mind. So many things happen nowadays, that out of sight is literally out of mind. Yet, now, when I think of it, I have an indistinct recollection of hearing that something had happened to Hardy—or was it that he had gone to England, he and his daughter ? "

Balmaine shook his head.

" They never came to England ! "

" You don't know that they never started though. As for that, I don't know either. But I know a man who can give you the information if anybody can ! "

" And that is——"

" Andrea Martino. He kept the Hotel Martino at Locarno, but that was only a blind. His house was really a rendezvous for revolutionists, and after 1866 he gave it up. But he knew everybody engaged in the revolutionary movement, and if anything happened to any of us he was sure to hear of it. Yes, I am certain that Martino could tell you what became of Hardy."

" Can you give me his address, Colonel ? "

" Unfortunately, I cannot. I have not seen him for two or three years. I met him accidentally at Naples, but though I did not ask him where he was living, I know he is not living there. I can get to know, though."

13*

"If you would kindly do so, Colonel Bevis, I should be very much obliged," Alfred said earnestly. "You will have to write to somebody, I suppose."

"I don't think writing would be any use. It must stand over until I make another trip into Italy."

Balmaine looked disappointed.

"When will that be?" he asked.

"In the winter; I am not sure what month. But you may be sure I shall not forget your commission. If you think there is any danger of my doing so (smiling), drop me a line about November. Here is my card."

The address on the card was Villa Italia, Nice.

"One question more, Colonel Bevis," said Alfred, putting the card into his pocket, "and I will cease troubling you. Do you know what *nom de guerre* Philip Hardy was in the habit of using?"

"I don't. I think he told me at Pallanza what he called himself just then, but I have quite forgotten whether it was Amelio, Fama, Frascati, or Leopardi. I rather fancy it was Leopardi. Martino will tell you in a moment."

"I wish I could see Martino a moment," muttered Balmaine despondingly. "I am going to have a short holiday, and almost think I shall cross the Alps and make some inquiries on my own account. Where would you recommend me to go?"

"About the Italian lakes and North Italy, I should say. That was generally Hardy's beat, I

think. And he was very fond of the Baths of Lucca.
The Baths of Lucca would be a likely place. But
unless you know under what name he went I don't
see what you can do. Better wait, and keep your
money in your pocket, until I can place you in communication with Martino."

"You could not possibly do that at once, could
you, Colonel?"

"How can I, when I have not the most remote
idea where the man is? I can find out from one or
other of my old comrades either at Turin or Milan,
or elsewhere; and if the man I ask does not happen
to know, he will certainly be able to tell me who
does. But as for writing, there is one absolute rule
these fellows make about letters, and that is never
to answer them."

Alfred, seeing it was useless to press the matter
further, let it drop, and shortly afterwards took his
leave, feeling both discouraged and disappointed;
for though the information he had obtained from
Bevis was good, so far as it went, it did not go far,
and it might be six months before he could be
placed in communication with Martino. Bevis
might surely get his address before that time if he
liked; and why did he not like? Then he was disappointed with the Colonel himself. Garibaldi was
Alfred's model hero, the type of all that was noble,
unselfish, and loyal. With that splendid disinte-
restedness he had given up his conquests to the

King; and, asking neither riches nor honours, re-
tired to his island home and resumed the cultivation
of his garden and the care of his cattle. The companion of such a man, "one of the few, the immortal
few that were not born to die," ought surely to have
imbibed something of his spirit, and to find in the
consciousness that he had followed a heroic leader
and fought in a great cause a reward far above deco-
rations and pelf. And yet here was Bevis grumbling
because Garibaldi had not done more for him than
he had done for himself, because he had not stooped
to entreat the Italian Government to recompense
the men who had redeemed a kingdom with their
blood! To blame the Liberator for this was to sur-
pass in meanness the Government which had failed
to perform so obvious a duty.

Yes, Alfred was disappointed with Bevis. The
fine old soldier, whom he had pictured in his imagination as a hero, was merely a smart and not very
scrupulous canvasser for advertisements, and now that
the novelty of the thing was wearing off he began to
perceive that most of the people whose acquaintance
he had lately made were, more or less, humbugs.
Furbey, Corfe, Gibson, Layland, Mayo, and Bevis
were every one humbugs, and the *Helvetic News* was
probably the biggest humbug of all. A few days
later, however, he saw reason to modify this judgment and assign the bad pre-eminence to the
Pitsburg Patriot. He had sent his bill to the pro-

prietor when he sent his last article to the editor;
and Dr. Pilgrim (who was a shining light of the
denomination to which he belonged) in acknowledg-
ing receipt of the two documents, wrote as follows:

"I am quite at a loss to understand how you can
have conceived the idea that we pay for contributions. If I may trust my memory (and it never yet
deceived me) nothing whatever was said about pay-
ment, and our friends are generally more than
satisfied with the consciousness that in writing for
us they are promoting a good cause, and the pleasure of seeing their compositions in print. Moreover, the Society which runs the *Patriot* is just now
far from rich, and cannot afford to use paid articles.
But as I cannot bear even the implied reproach of
having misled you, however inadvertently, I shall
send you in the course of a few days the sum of five
dollars, being at the rate of one dollar an article,
which I trust you will deem in the circumstances a
fair equivalent for your trouble."

This was a bitter disappointment to Alfred in
more ways than one, for counting confidently on
getting his money from the *Patriot*, he had spent
rather more freely than he otherwise would have
done, and had hardly any money beforehand either
for holiday making or contingencies. To make
matters worse the *Boston Hub*, for which he had

written three letters, paid him in the same coin as the *Pitsburg Patriot.* In reply to his request to fill up the " blank bill " he sent them, with whatever amount they thought he deserved, the proprietors observed that, having a good many amateur correspondents in Europe, they were not in the habit of paying for foreign letters, but if he would continue his contributions (which seemed to please their readers) they would be happy to mail him regularly a free copy of their bi-weekly edition.

" What a mean lot of beggars they are ! " was Balmaine's exclamation as he tore up the letter with unnecessary energy, and threw the bits on the floor. " This is my first experience of American papers and, by Jove, it shall be my last."

But he found that if an American journal can be mean, an American gentleman can do all that the most scrupulous regard for honour requires. A few days afterwards he met Harman, and the banker, who was always very friendly, after asking about himself and the paper, inquired how he was getting on with the *Pitsburg Patriot.* For reply Alfred showed him Dr. Pilgrim's letter.

" The wretched old skunk ! " exclaimed Harman, giving the letter a blow with his fist, as if it were in some way answerable for the dishonesty of the writer. " Why, I heard him say myself that he would pay you at the rate of twenty dollars a letter. But look here, Balmaine, I introduced this fellow to

you, and recommended you to write for him, and I'll
see you paid."

He was as good as his word. The very next day
Alfred received a letter from the bank, enclosing a
bank note for five hundred francs, and this sum, as
he afterwards learnt, Harman's agents succeeded in
recovering from Dr. Pilgrim.

Of all his new acquaintance Balmaine liked best
to talk with Madame Karl von Schmidt. She had
seen a good deal of the world, possessed a shrewd
wit, the vicissitudes she had undergone made her
sympathetic with the troubles of others, and she
took a motherly interest in his welfare. Delane,
however, she generally kept at a distance, perhaps
because she wanted to keep him at a distance from
her daughter.

Madame Karl took hardly less interest in the
Hardy mystery than Alfred himself, and he had to
give her a full account of his conversation with
Bevis, which had so greatly disappointed him. She
hinted, much to his surprise, that if he offered to
pay the Colonel for his trouble he would probably
find him more communicative. It was not very
noble or chivalrous on his part, she said, " but you
must take people as you find them." And Bevis
knew the value of money—a good many people did
not.

" I am learning," laughed Balmaine. " I have
learned a great deal since I left home. I get more

disillusioné every day. I shall think soon, with Napoleon, that every man has his price."

" Then you will be wrong. Most men have—but not all. As you say, you are learning, and there is no teacher like experience. But as for this mystery of yours I must tell you frankly, Monsieur Balmaine, that I think you are making very good progress. You have met a man who knew Monsieur Hardy and his daughter, who confirms that they were in Italy at a certain time, and who promises to give you the address of a person who can give you his *nom de guerre*, and tell you what became of him. I do not see what you would have more— unless you expect to read all about it in the *Journal de Lacustrie*, at a cost of fifteen centimes. A mystery that can be solved by asking six questions, *ma foi*, I would not give a fig for."

" You are right, Madame Karl; I am too impatient, and I was so much annoyed at not getting Martino's address that I overlooked the importance of the information I have actually acquired. I must now see what I can do about offering Colonel Bevis something for his trouble."

The next day Alfred wrote to Artful and Higginbottom, announcing his intention of making a journey across the Alps in quest of information. He told them, too, what he had learnt from Bevis, and asked if they would permit him to offer that gentleman an *honorarium* for the trouble he might incur in obtaining Martino's address.

The answer was a letter highly commending his exertions, and urging him to persevere, and to spare no effort to procure Martino's address. A draft for fifty pounds was enclosed, " to be used for travelling expenses, or otherwise, at your discretion."

But before the letter came Bevis was gone ; and though Balmaine wrote to him at once his movements were so uncertain, and he was so bad a correspondent, that, as likely as not, the reply might be delayed for weeks.

CHAPTER XXIII.

MADEMOISELLE LEONINO.

"WHO will go to the inaugural fête of the Hôtel Rousseau?" said Gibson one morning, as he came into the sub-editor's room with two large, gaily got-up cards in his hand. "That big hotel at the other end of the lake, you know. I dare say it will be a very grand affair. The proprietors want something saying about it, I suppose; and as they have given us a good advertisement we must try to oblige them. Will you go, Balmaine?"

"Certainly," said Alfred. "It will be a new experience, and, I have no doubt, a very pleasant one."

"I am sure it will; and as these people want a notice they are sure to make much of you. But here's a second ticket. Will you go too, Delane? I dare say we can spare you both for a day."

"No, I thank you, Mr. Gibson. There will be dancing; I don't dance, and, to tell the truth, I have not such a thing as a dress-coat."

"Would Milnthorpe go, do you think?"

"I am sure he wouldn't. I don't think he has

more than one pair of shoes, and they are bursting in all directions. You must send somebody who will be a credit to the paper."

" But Milnthorpe is not so desperately poor as all that comes to. I have got his salary raised to fifty francs. It is not much, perhaps, but it should afford a new pair of shoes."

" I cannot make Milnthorpe out," observed Delane thoughtfully. " From the way he lives, he should not be spending more than twenty francs a week. He is saving money; that's what Milnthorpe is doing. I wish I could save some."

As this remark was made the door opened, and Corfe appeared on the scene.

" Perhaps Corfe will have the second ticket," said Gibson. " Will you, Corfe ? "

" If it's anything very jolly, I say yes, with thanks," was the answer.

Gibson explained.

" I cannot do much dancing with this game leg of mine, but I suppose they will put us up and give us something to eat and drink ! "

" Not a doubt of it—something very good too, I should say."

" Then I will go. 1 dare say I can while away the time somehow while Balmaine is doing the light fantastic," said Corfe laughing at his own conceit, " and a fellow can always smoke, you know."

" It is understood that we go together, then," put in Alfred ; " by water, of course ? "

" Of course.   Going by water is a delight, by rail an infliction—heaven and hell.   I vote for heaven. We meet at the *embarcadère*—at what time ? "

" I think we had better go by the two o'clock boat."

" I shall be there.   It will bring us just in time for the table d'hôte.   And now I must be off and arrange about my lessons.   *Au revoir.*"

" Corfe seems to be in good spirits to-day," remarked Gibson as the door closed.

" Very much so.   He is rather freer with his money, too, than he was a little while ago.   Perhaps he has got another good paying-pupil.   I wonder who that ill-looking Italian is that he talks so much with at the Café du Roi ? "

" Why don't you ask him ? "

" No, thank you.   If you show too much curiosity about Corfe's private affairs he has a way of dropping on you that is not very agreeable, and I don't want to fall out with him."

Whatever may have been Corfe's faults of temper, or otherwise, he showed none of them on the voyage up the lake.   He chatted pleasantly all the way, and his manner to Alfred was so cordial that the latter almost resolved that, as they went back, he would ask him whether, during his travels in Italy, he had heard or seen anything of the Hardys.

His family had been in the habit of visiting the Baths of Lucca every year. Vera was born at Lucca, and, as appeared from Philip's letter, they had often been there since. What more likely than that Corfe should know something of them? At any rate, there could be no harm in asking him, and, if a good opportunity offered, he could put the question as they returned. He might put it now, but experience was making Alfred cautious. He did not want to take Corfe too much into his confidence, or let him know the extent of the Hardy fortune. It would be better, he thought, to introduce the subject as it were accidentally, and apropos of something else. To lug it in by the head and shoulders might excite Corfe's suspicion, and cause him to keep something back, as Bevis had done; for, besides being half Italian by education, Corfe was quite as sharp as the Colonel, and probably less scrupulous.

They arrived, as they expected, just in time for dinner, and were treated by the proprietor of the hotel with a politeness so excessive, with so much bowing and scraping and offers of this, that, and the other, that Alfred was half amused, half annoyed; but Corfe evidently liked it, bowed condescendingly to the master, and ordered the servants about as if he owned them. Everybody thought he was the proprietor of the *Helvetic News* and Balmaine his secretary.

At dinner the head waiter asked Corfe, with

much deference, what wine they would have, whereupon Corfe ordered first a bottle of old Margaux and then a bottle of Napoleon Cabinet. This annoyed Alfred.

"These people are giving us a good dinner," he said, "and treating us otherwise very handsomely. It seems hardly fair to drink their most expensive wines."

"They will respect you all the more for it," replied Corfe with an air of calm superiority. "I know these people better than you do, my dear fellow. If we ordered *vin ordinaire* and Swiss gooseberry they would set us down as fools. And it is a good rule to take of the best when you have the chance. You remember the Irishman's advice to his son—'Never drink water when you can drink wine, and never kiss the maid when you can kiss the mistress.' This Margaux is a very fair wine. We shall be able to tell our friends, Jules" (turning to the head waiter), "that the Hôtel Rousseau is starting with an excellent cellar."

"Oui, monsieur, we have some very good wine It is only old-established hotels that can afford to give their guests inferior *crues*. We have also some superb liqueurs—cognac fifty years old. Would monsieur like to have a *petit verre* of it?"

"I think I would. Bring me one after the fish. Will you have one, Balmaine?"

Alfred declined. He did not know whether to be

amused with Corfe's *aplomb* or vexed with his assurance.

After dinner they went into the garden and watched, while they smoked, the completion of the preparations for the fête. The Hôtel Rousseau was finely situated in the grounds of an ancient château, of which the central part had been preserved, and ingeniously incorporated into the new structure, built in the same style of architecture, and the old tower being covered with ivy, the general effect was pleasing and picturesque. The house was long and double fronted, approached on one side by a magnificent double avenue of chestnut-trees, and on the other by a broad flight of steps, which led directly from the lake. On the opposite shore a huge mountain, its black and splintered summit powdered with fresh-fallen snow, rose sheer from the water, while behind it Alp was piled on Alp, each loftier than the other, until the last was lost in the evening haze. The landward front faced a range of vine-clad slopes, dotted with fairy-like villas, green meadows sweeping upwards towards dark pine-woods, and naked promontories of rock, which seemed to be hanging in mid-air.

Then the curtain of night fell; the ivy-clad tower glowed with hidden fires, the entire front of the hotel was illuminated, the Chinese lanterns that hung among the trees were lighted up, some of the

larger trees carrying a lantern on every branch.
There were fountains in which Neptunes and mer-
maids bore flaming torches above fleeting rain-
bows; and two lines of boats, each with a lantern
fore and aft, and rising and falling with the
swell of the lake, made a waterway nearly a mile
long. The effect was weird, charming, and fantastic; the Rousseau gardens had been converted
into fairyland, and "when music rose with its
voluptuous swell," Balmaine felt like dancing all
over.

"Come along!" he exclaimed with honest
enthusiasm; "let us walk round. I never saw
anything like this before."

"It's not so bad for Switzerland," returned Corfe
with a half-sneer. "But you should see the *fêtes
des fleurs* at Nice, or Versailles illuminated, and the
grand fountains playing."

"Bother Versailles and its grand fountains!
What is Versailles, with its stucco and paint and
square-cut gardens to compare with those mountains
and this lake? The Chinese lanterns don't amount
to much, perhaps; but the scene altogether is
superb."

"Are you going to dance?" asked Corfe, who
seemed rather taken aback by this outburst.

"If I can get a partner I will, certainly. Who
could resist that music?"

"I'll get you a partner fast enough. Come

this way. Isn't that Fastnacht (one of the managers)?"

"Can I do anything for you, gentlemen?" said Fastnacht, rubbing his hands deferentially and making a low bow. "I hope you like the illumination."

"My friend——" began Corfe.

"The illumination is superb, M. Fastnacht," broke in Alfred—he was beginning to resent Corfe's continual patronage. "I think I never saw anything so beautiful. I have been watching it for some time, and now I feel as if I should like a dance. Do you think you could find me a partner?"

"Perfectly, M. Balmaine, as many as you like. Will you give yourself the trouble to step this way?"

The avenue of chestnut-trees was fitted up as a ball-room. Boards were laid on the space reserved for the dancers, the orchestra being partitioned off by a low curtain of red drapery; and the flags of Switzerland, England, the United States, and other nationalities, were festooned in graceful folds from tree to tree.

Fastnacht led Balmaine to a group composed of a middle-aged lady and gentleman and two or three young girls.

"How do you do, M. Senarclens?" said the manager. "Behold M. Balmaine, an English

14*

gentleman from Geneva; he would very much like to dance. Perhaps one of your young ladies would oblige him ? "

"Not a doubt of it," returned M. Senarclens pleasantly. "Here is Mademoiselle Leonino; I am sure she will be happy to dance with monsieur."

Balmaine, bowing to the demoiselle thus designated, asked in his best French if she would do him the pleasure. The demoiselle smiled, rose, bowed, and the next moment they were whirling among the Chinese lanterns at the rate of ten miles an hour. Alfred had seen at once that his partner was a sweet and graceful girl; but it was only when he was leading her back to her friends that he had an opportunity of examining her in detail, waltzing not being favourable to minute observation.

Mademoiselle Leonino was tall, slim, and well-shaped, but perhaps rather too square-shouldered. Her oval, slightly olive-tinted and sunburnt face was mobile and expressive, lighted up with a pair of bright black eyes, and surmounted with a mass of golden hair—some would have called it red; but red or golden, no fitter setting could have been desired for the girl's winsome and intelligent countenance.

But she seemed to have no tongue, and though he asked her several questions and made sundry remarks, she answered nothing save yea and nay.

"That is a deuced nice girl you have been dancing with," said Corfe, when he next met his companion; "who is she?"

"Except that she is with a certain M. Senarclens and that her name is Leonino, I cannot tell you."

"Leonino is an Italian name, and she has an Italian look, too. But there are lots of people in this part of Switzerland with Italian names. I know half-a-dozen myself. Yes, she is a very pretty girl. I like red hair, don't you?"

"If you call that red hair, I don't; I call it golden."

Balmaine danced with several other demoiselles in the course of the evening, but he liked his first partner so well that he danced with her twice again, and would have danced with her a fourth time if she and her friends had not suddenly disappeared.

On the second occasion she was less reserved. She answered some of his questions, and even made one or two original observations. On the third occasion he ventured to ask her, in a roundabout fashion, where she lived.

"I suppose you live in this neighbourhood?" he said.

"My home is up there in the mountains," she replied, pointing towards the Waadtland Alps.

"It must be very lonely. Do you like your life up there?"

"I love the mountains, oh, so much! What would life be without them?" she answered eagerly. "Even in winter they are glorious; more glorious, I sometimes think, than in summer. But mountains are not all; there are other things——" and then a shadow fell over her face, and she stopped abruptly, as if she feared that she might be committing an indiscretion.

Alfred would have liked to ask her what the other things were, but that, he felt, might be presuming too much, and he asked her instead whether she ever went to Geneva.

"I have only been there once," was the answer. "I rarely leave home, and should not have come to the fête if M. Senarclens had not asked me."

"M. Senarclens! Is he the great M. Senarclens of whom one has heard?"

"Yes, he is the great French historian. He lives down there by the lake, but in the summer he comes up to the mountains."

"But you are not French?"

"No, I am not French. I don't know exactly what I am. My father was——"

"Pardon, Monsieur. I hope you have enjoyed yourself, and you also, Mademoiselle. The fête is a great success, I think. The dancing will now cease for half an hour for the display of fireworks. You will see it best from the terrace."

The speaker was the indefatigable Fastnacht, and

almost at the same moment Madame Senarclens
came up, and Alfred saw no more of Mademoiselle
Leonino that night, nor for some time thereafter.
Another moment and she would have told him that
her father was English and her mother Italian, and
he would have known that the girl by his side was
her whom he sought—Philip Hardy's daughter.

In the rush for the terrace, Balmaine lost sight of
the Senarclens, and though he sought for them
afterwards they were nowhere to be found. He
danced a few times more, but with little spirit or
enjoyment. The glamour of the fête seemed to be
passed, the candles in the Chinese lanterns began to
gutter and go out, the music grew less lively; he
noticed for the first time that some vulgar men and
tawdry-dressed women were among the dancers, and
that several of the guests appeared to have taken
more wine than was good for them. So without
saying anything to Corfe, who was playing at cards
in the hotel smoking-room, he went quietly off to
bed, wondering what Mademoiselle Leonino would
have said if she had not been interrupted, for the
expression, " I am not French; I don't know exactly
what I am," was too singular to be easily forgotten.

Corfe came down very late to breakfast next
morning, but in excellent humour, due probably to
the fact, which he imparted to Alfred, that he had
" picked up " several napoleons at play. But as he
did not want to impress the young fellow unfavour-

ably, or have it known at the office that he had
been gambling, he said whist, albeit the game was
baccarat.

" Did you see any more of that pretty girl with
the red hair and black eyes ? " he asked. " Leonino,
isn't she called ? "

" Very little," said Balmaine, rather coldly.
" She went away early. I saw nothing of her after
the fireworks."

" I should not wonder if she belonged to one of
those Swiss families of Italian origin that settled in
Switzerland about the time of the Reformation.
She has evidently both Northern and Southern
blood in her veins. I do not think I ever saw such
a combination of blonde and brunette in the same
person. Yes, Mademoiselle Leonino is very good-
looking. I wish I knew where she lived."

There was something in the manner in which this
was said, even more than the words themselves,
that grated on Alfred's feelings. He did not like
to discuss Mademoiselle Leonino with Corfe, but as
he had no right to resent the remark, even had it
been expedient to do so, he said something about
its being nearly time to start, lighted a cigar, and
strolled out on the terrace.

Half an hour later they were speeding towards
Geneva. The sun was right above them, and Balmaine was watching the effect of light and shade
on the hills and dales of the Savoyard side, and

wondering when—if ever—he should have the
opportunity of climbing the glaciers which crowned
the summits of the Pennine Alps, and looking down
from them on the historic land of which he had
heard and read so much.

" I wish I were on the other side," says Corfe,
pointing to Mont Blanc.

" You like Italy ? "

" Better than any other country. If some good
soul would leave me five hundred a year—a fellow
may exist on five hundred a year in Italy—I should
live nowhere else. You have not been to Chamouni
yet ? "

" No."

" You must go. I have been there several times.
I once crossed over the Col du Géant to Courmayeur,
and then footed it to Turin. That was one of the
pleasantest tramps I ever had. You should go to
Italy, Balmaine."

" I am going."

" Soon ? "

" In a few days, I think."

" It is a bad time now ; too hot. You should
wait till September, or better still, October."

" I must go when I can get off, and I rather like
heat."

" You will get what you like, then. You won't
take much harm, though, if you keep about the
lakes."

" That is what I mean to do, but I should like to see Turin, Milan, and one or two other places. I want to make a few inquiries about a missing Englishman, though I do not suppose it will be of much use."

" A missing Englishman ! Who is he—a relative of yours ? "

" Oh, dear, no. Some people I know are anxious to ascertain what has become of him. He lived in Italy, and has not been heard of for ten years or more."

" What is his name ? I may perhaps have met him or heard of him. I used to meet a good many English when I was in Italy."

" His name was Hardy."

" Was he married ? "

" At one time ; but when last heard of he was a widower, with a little girl about seven years old."

Alfred said, further, that Philip Hardy went sometimes under another name, mentioned the places he was in the habit of frequenting, and a few other facts.

" Hardy ! " said Corfe thoughtfully, " I don't think I ever knew anybody of that name, at any rate in Italy. I suppose the aliases he used were Italian ? "

" I should think so."

" Is there money in it ? " asked Corfe abruptly, after a long pause, which seemed to be grave and reflective.

Alfred looked as if he did not quite understand. Corfe was drawing conclusions much faster than he liked, and he wanted time to think.

" I was merely thinking why these people you speak of are so anxious to find him. I have lived long enough in the world to know that when a man who has been missing ten years is wanted, money is generally at the bottom of it."

" Money is not my motive, at any rate. It is partly curiosity, partly a desire to oblige a friend. Whether Philip Hardy be alive or dead I am not likely to profit a penny. Most people think he is dead."

" And if he is, who will get his money ? "

" It is a question whether he had any money. If he died before his father he had none."

" Did these Hardys live in London ? "

" Yes."

" When did the old man die ? "

" John Hardy died about ten years ago. But I really don't see what all this has to do with it, Corfe. I don't want you to take any trouble in the matter. I thought you might possibly have met Hardy somewhere, more especially as the Baths of Lucca seem to have been a favourite resort of his, and you were often there, you say."

" I don't think I ever met anybody called Hardy, either at Lucca or elsewhere, and you don't know his Italian name.   Have you any idea what he was like ? "

" I never saw him, or even a portrait of him ; but he has been described to me as a handsome, powerfully-built man, rather above middle height, with reddish hair and beard, light complexion and blue eyes, and a look half-soldier, half-artist."

" And he had a little girl with him ? "

" Yes, but what she was like I have no idea."

" No," said Corfe, slowly, as if he was searching every nook and cranny of his memory.   " No, I cannot tell you anything about them.   Never met a man and a little girl like that, I am sure ; and I don't think there is the least chance of finding a clue—unless you can ascertain by what name they generally went."

So Balmaine learnt nothing whatever from Corfe, and he could not help thinking that he had possibly made a mistake in mooting the matter to him ; yet why should he think so ?   Albeit Alfred had told him more than he intended, Corfe had, after all, not got to know very much ; moreover the facts concerning the Hardy fortune were no secret ; whoever chose to take a little trouble could easily learn all about the case.   If Corfe thought he had some sinister motive in making the inquiry, what then ?   He cared nothing about Corfe.   Yet though Balmaine argued thus, he could not shake off the vague feeling of uneasiness with which the con-

versation had inspired him. He did not like the
keen way in which Corfe had questioned him, and
his eagerness to know if "there was money in it"
was not pleasant. No harm might come of it—he
did not see how there could—but for all that he
wished he had kept his own counsel.

CHAPTER XXIV

CORFE IS CURIOUS.

TEN days later Balmaine started for Lucerne, *en route* for Italy, and almost at the same hour Corfe called on an *avocat* who was much consulted by members of the English colony. His object was to inquire if the *avocat* had an agent in London, and on receiving an answer in the affirmative, he instructed him to obtain an abstract of the will of John Hardy, who had lived in London and died there about ten years before. If the will of more than one John Hardy should be found at Doctor's Commons, the agent was to send abstracts of each of them.

"I am sure that beggar Balmaine did not tell me everything," muttered Corfe, as he left the *avocat's étude.* "We shall soon see whether there is money in it or not—money is at the bottom of everything in this world I think, or ought to be. If there is, I shall try to profit by the opportunity. No, no, Mr. Balmaine, you don't pick my brains for nothing—not if I know it. I do believe it is the same. That description answers perfectly to the

Leonino we knew at Lucca—little girl and all. If it had not been for that girl Balmaine danced with, though, I should never have known. The moment I heard her name it seemed to recall something, but I could not tell what—one may forget a good deal in twelve years. But when Balmaine described what sort of fellow. Hardy was it all came back to me. He was rather friendly with my father, I remember, and one evening when we were leaving the Café Cartoni—that was in Lucca itself—the governor whispered to me, as a sort of secret, that Leonino, in spite of his Italian name, was an Englishman, and member of a revolutionary society, and afterwards I saw him and his little girl and her *bonne* walking on the ramparts, and again at the baths. I have not a doubt he is the very man Balmaine is inquiring about, any more than I have that he is as dead as Moses. I suppose they want to prove the fact in order that somebody may get hold of his leavings. Well, if they want my help they must pay for it, that is all. I shall know more when I get a copy of the old man's will, if he made a will. By-the-bye, Balmaine said very little about the girl—she must be a woman by this time. If the father is dead she will inherit, naturally. Oh, oh, Mr. Balmaine, I see what you are after; you are after the daughter. But after all this time you won't find it easy to trace her, I'm thinking. I did not ask him her Christian name, that was a mistake.

I wonder—no, the thing would be too absurd, and Leonino is not an uncommon name. Mademoiselle Leonino is a very fine girl all the same, and I mean to cultivate her acquaintance. Fastnacht asked me to go down again and spend a few days at the Rousseau. I have half a mind to go on Saturday and stay till Monday. And when I get the abstract of the will what shall I do?—write to the trustees or heirs-at-law, or whoever they are?—they can be found out, I suppose—and ask them to give me the job of finding out what has become of this man— and I'll make 'em pay too."

On this idea Corfe acted; the following Saturday he revisited the Rousseau, and for two days lorded it over the servants and lived on the fat of the land. He liked hotel life, and had it been in his power would have lived in hotels altogether. When he asked Fastnacht about Mademoiselle Leonino the manager gave him a knowing look.

"A fine girl, isn't she?" he said; "a very fine girl. You are not the first man by any means, Mr. Corfe, who has asked questions about Mademoiselle Vera Leonino."

"She is called Vera, is she?"

"Yes."

"And she lives at Clarens, I suppose, or is it Vevey?"

"Neither; she lives up in the mountains, near a village called—let me see—I forget just now, but I shall remember afterwards, and if I don't I can get to know for you."

" Who are her people ? "

" Peasants."

" Nonsense. She has quite a lady-like air and good manners."

" It does seem rather strange, doesn't it ? But it is what M. Senarclens was telling me on the night of the fête. I am afraid, though, I had my head too full of other things to pay proper attention to all he said. But the peasant family she lives with are no relatives."

" No ! "

" No, the daughter was her *bonne* when she was quite a little thing, and Mademoiselle Vera's father left her in the *bonne's* charge, and money enough to pay for her bringing up."

" A strange story," said Corfe, who began to see that he was in a fair way for making an important discovery. " What is the *bonne's* name ? "

" That I forget, too ; but if you like I will inform myself."

" Thank you," said Corfe carelessly. " I wish you would—when you have an opportunity—if it is not too much trouble."

Corfe's idea in going to the Rousseau a second time had been simply to spend a day or two pleasantly and, if he could, make the acquaintance of Mademoiselle Leonino, a design that boded the girl no good, for he had strong passions and few scruples. But the story told him by M. Fastnacht suggested quite a new order of ideas. The theory which he had conceived, only to dismiss as absurd, that Mademoiselle Leonino was the daughter of the man he had met at Lucca, and whom Balmaine was so anxious to find, seemed now plausible enough. The girl lived with a family of peasants, to whom she was in no way akin; her father had left her in charge of her *bonne,* probably the very *bonne* that he had seen at Lucca; and, finally, her name was Leonino. True, these might be merely fortuitous coincidences, and Mademoiselle Leonino not the daughter of Philip Hardy after all. On the other hand, the matter was well worth inquiring into, and when Fastnacht had got to know with whom the girl lived and where, he would go forthwith and look her and the *bonne* up. But he was too crafty to press Fastnacht—he did not want the manager to suppose that he had any other motives than idle curiosity and admiration of the girl's beauty; and as Fastnacht, being much occupied with his own affairs, quite forgot to make the promised inquiry, Corfe, much to his chagrin, was obliged to leave without learning anything further. But he resolved to return on an early day and by hook or crook find out what he wanted to know.

Shortly afterwards the abstract of John Hardy's will arrived. The reading of it seemed to set

Corfe's brain on fire. When he saw that the personalty had been sworn under £800,000, and that there was much landed property in addition, all left to "my son Philip," and that Philip being dead, his daughter would inherit all this wealth, he felt for a moment as if the emotions that swept through his mind, and the golden dreams which rose tumultuously before his mental vision would suffocate him. This vast fortune was before his eyes—nearly within his grasp!

"Why," he almost shouted, "why should I not marry this girl before she knows herself how rich she is, and so become at one stroke a millionaire— a millionaire, not in beggarly francs, but in pounds sterling! Heavens! what might not a man do with a million—twenty-five million, perhaps fifty million francs!"

But was this girl he had seen at the Rousseau really and beyond any sort of doubt Philip Hardy's daughter? That was the question. If so, why should she be living with a family of peasants in a remote Swiss village? There was a story behind all this; what could it be? He must ascertain, and he could only ascertain by personal inquiry in the place where Mademoiselle Leonino lived. Not yet, however; circumspection was now more necessary than ever, and to present himself at the Rousseau before a reasonable time had elapsed, and without any other apparent motive than to ask where the

15*

girl lived, might excite suspicion, and his game
was to keep the facts, his suspicions, asbolutely
to himself. If Mademoiselle Leonino were to find
out that she was a great heiress it might not be so
easy for him to marry her. The foster child of a
Swiss *bonne* was one thing, a millionaire maiden
quite another. There were good reasons, moreover,
why he should keep himself in the background and
his whereabouts unknown. Yes, he must remain
in Geneva and keep quiet until, at any rate, that
beggar Balmaine came back. He was a straight-
forward, unsuspicious young fellow, and it would not
be difficult to ascertain from him the Christian
name of Philip Hardy's daughter, without letting it
be seen that he had any particular object in making
the inquiry. If it were "Vera" there could not be
a shadow of a doubt that Vera Leonino and Vera
Hardy were one and the same person. His next
move would be to find out where she lived, and
make her acquaintance. It would not be difficult,
he thought, to persuade a girl in her position to
accept an English gentleman of good family,
willing to take her without a portion. As to that
he had no fear; he was always successful with
women, and girls of seventeen or eighteen were
great fools; they believed everything you told
them.

So Corfe awaited with what patience he might
Balmaine's return but there was hardly a day on

which he did not call at the office of the *Helvetic* to
inquire when the assistant editor was likely to be
back, hardly an hour that he did not mentally
curse the young fellow's dilatoriness. The prospect
of coming into a million sterling, possibly twice as
much, for in the circumstances there would naturally
be no question of settlements, excited him almost
beyond endurance. "To miss it," he said to himself, grinding his teeth and clenching his hands at
the mere thought, " would be hell."

How, meanwhile, was Balmaine faring? As
touching the main object of his journey badly
enough, yet hardly worse than he expected, for he
did not disguise from himself that, after so long a
time, and ignorant as he was of Hardy's aliases, the
chance of finding a clue was exceedingly remote.
On that chance he went, and if it failed him he
should be in no worse position than before. He
would still have Bevis and Martino to fall back
upon, and in justice both to Warton and Artful
and Higginbottom he was bound to do his best.

After walking over the St. Gothard, as well for
reasons of economy, as the better to survey the
scenes of the campaign of 1799 in which he took
a great interest, Alfred changed to wheels at Airolo,
and descended the gorges of the Ticino to the
shores of Lago Maggiore on the top of a diligence.
It was one of the pleasantest bits of travel he had
ever enjoyed, and when the lake in all its un-

matched loveliness rolled out before him he was in
an ecstasy of delight.   He saw evidence everywhere
that he had crossed the Alps.   Though the mountains were the same, the landscape was softer, and
the vegetation different.   The vines were trained
in another fashion, the hills were rounder and more
wooded, the buildings more spacious, the people
more picturesque.   At Locarno he stayed all night,
and made a few fruitless inquiries.   The Hotel
Martino no longer existed; the money-changer
who had cashed Philip Hardy's drafts was dead,
and when he asked mine host of the inn at which he
put up, if he had ever heard of an English gentleman of the name of Hardy, who frequently visited
Locarno some ten or twelve years previously, the man,
who belonged to canton Uri, told him that he had
lived in Locarno but six years, and recommended
him to see the postmaster, an old fellow who had
lived there all his life.   The postmaster, whose
temper seemed none of the sweetest, said that
during the last thirty years he had seen and spoken
to about a hundred thousand Englishmen, who were
either staying in or passing through Locarno, that
he did not remember the name of one of them, and
had never heard the name of Hardy before.

Balmaine almost laughed at himself for asking
so absurd a question, and only the feeing that it
was his duty to make an effort to earn his travelling
expenses induced him to go on.   But it was the

same everywhere else, and at Milan he came to
the conclusion that unless he could obtain an
introduction to some old revolutionist, and devote
months to the task, it would be useless to persevere. He even abandoned his intention of
going to Lucca, which in one respect was a misfortune, for if he had heard nothing about Philip
Hardy he might have heard something about
Vernon Corfe which would have been almost as
valuable.

He returned over the Simplon, and from Domo
d'Ossola wrote to Artful and Higginbottom, ap-
prising them of his failure, expressing the opinion
that until he could see Martino there was no use
attempting anything anything further, and adding
that he expected to have news of him through
Colonel Bevis on his arrival at Geneva. He did in
effect find a letter from the Colonel at his lodgings,
but it contained nothing very satisfactory. Bevis
said he was much obliged for Alfred's offer to defray
any expenses he might incur in prosecuting the inquiry about Martino, and that he would forward particulars of what he might spend in due course. As
for obtaining his address, he could only repeat that
it was quite impossible for him to do so until he
went to Italy. He would if he could, but it was
really quite out of his power.

With this assurance Alfred was obliged to be con-
tent. There was nothing for it but to possess his

soul in patience and wait.   The day after his return
he met Corfe on the Island Bridge.

" When did you get back ? " says Corfe in his most
affable manner.

" Last night."

" I hope you enjoyed yourself."

" Thank you.   I enjoyed the journey immensely,
though it was so warm."

" Did you go to Venice ? "

" No."

" What a pity ! You should not have missed the
Queen of the Adriatic on any account.   However,
you are sure to go to Italy again. Nobody ever visits
Italy once without wanting to see it a second time.
How did you succeed with your quest ? "

" Not at all."

" You have heard nothing of the missing Mr.
Hardy, then ? "

" Nothing."

" Nor of his daughter, the missing Miss What's-
her-name.   You did tell me, I think, but I forget."

" Vera."

" Ah ! "   Try as he would, Corfe could not keep
down that exclamation, nor prevent the blood from
rushing to his head and suffusing his face.

" What ? " asks Alfred, with a look of surprise.

" I was struck with the coincidence, that's all,"
returns Corfe with admirable presence of mind.
" One of my sisters is called Vera ; strange, isn't

it. I was afraid you wouldn't succeed when you told me about it. So many things may happen in ten years, you know. In my opinion, both father and daughter are either dead or lost for ever. However, if I can do anything to help you have only to speak. I will do my best."

Alfred thanked him, and then each went his way.

"It is all right, no mistake this time," thought Corfe exultantly, as he leaned on the parapet of the bridge and watched the Rhone as it swept clear and blue towards the rapids of St Jean. "She is the Vera, my Vera, for she shall be mine, let who will say nay. I'll go to the Rousseau on Saturday, and make old Fastnacht tell me where she is, and before two months are over I'll marry her; and then won't I astonish some of their weak nerves ? "

But there was a mistake this time, and before two days were over Corfe experienced the truth of the adage that there's many a slip between the cup and the lip.

CHAPTER XXV

AN UNEXPECTED ARRIVAL.

"WHAT sort of a post had you this morning?" asked Gibson one afternoon, as he passed through the sub-editor's room to his own. This was a more important question than it may seem, for the extent of an editor's correspondence is no bad sign of the influence of his paper.

"Very fair," answered Delane, whose duty it was to open all letters directed to the editor; "but there is a letter here which I did not venture to open. It is marked private."

"From a woman," said the editor, tearing open the envelope. "Poetry, I suppose, with a private appeal for favourable consideration. No, it isn't. Queer, this! What do you make of it, Delane?" (throwing the letter on the sub-editors' table). "It is about your friend Corfe."

The letter, which was dated from London, ran as follows:

"DEAR SIR,—May I ask you to do me a slight favour, for which I shall be greatly obliged, and tender you my best thanks beforehand. I believe that Mr. Vernon Corfe is at present in Geneva and a contributor to your paper. If he is *not*, kindly let me know at your earliest convenience. If, on the other hand, he is at Geneva, you need not take the trouble to write. I shall consider your silence as equivalent to a reply in the affirmative.

" Yours faithfully,

" ESTHER CORFE."

" What do I make of it ? " replied Delane. " It is from somebody who wants to know whether Corfe is here or not."

" How very sharp we are ! You should have been a detective, Delane. Your talents are quite thrown away as a journalist. The fact is, I suppose, you don't want to give an opinion. But have you no idea who this Esther Corfe is ? "

" His sister, I should say, or his mother."

" Is it possible, do you think, that his people are ignorant of his whereabouts ? "

" I should not wonder. Corfe is rather a strange fellow, and from hints he has occasionally dropped, I fancy he is not on the best of terms with his family."

" That is likely enough, I should say. He does not seem to have a very angelic temper. Or this lady may be his wife."

" Oh no, that is out of the question."

" Why is it out of the question ? "

" I never heard him say that he was married."

" That proves nothing. Many a man has run away from his wife before now, and if it be so with Corfe he is not likely to tell you anything about it. I shall watch for the *dénouement* with curiosity."

"Will you take any notice of the letter ? "

" Why should I ?   Corfe being here no answer is required."

" You won't say anything about it to him ? "

" Certainly not ; why should I ? Nor to anybody else, and I would not advise you to do either."

" I shall take care I don't.   He would very likely take it amiss.   Not that I don't always get on very well with him, but he is a very nasty fellow to fall out with."

The *dénouement* anticipated by Gibson was not long in coming to pass.

A fortnight later, that is to say, exactly two days after Alfred's return from Italy, a *voiture*, with a big box outside and a young woman inside, was driven up to the office of the *Helvetic News*, whereupon the *cocher*, descending very deliberately from his seat (he was rather fat) opened the carriage door.

"*Voici, madame, le bureau du journal anglais!*" he says in a husky voice, and his breath is unpleasantly suggestive of absinthe and garlic.

On this his fare, gathering her skirts about her,

alights cleverly on the *trottoir* and enters the business department of the paper. She is perhaps twenty-five years old, and neatly, but far from extravagantly dressed. The cast of her features is Jewish, and though her cheeks are hollow and her expression careworn, she has evidently been a handsome woman and is still eminently good-looking. Those large and occasionally flashing dark eyes, that mass of lustrous black hair would redeem any face however insignificant from the charge of plainness, and this young woman's face is both intelligent and refined, a face that wins on you, and, when she smiles, of a Madonna-like sweetness.

Pushing open the great swinging door of the office rather timidly, she finds herself before a wide mahogany counter and in the immediate presence of a hairy-faced and spectacled young man, who is smoking a cigarette and turning over the leaves of a very big visitors' book.

"I beg pardon," she says timidly, "do you speak English?"

"Dees is an English newspaper, Madame, and we all naturally speaks ze English langvidge," answers the young man feelingly, as if he was hurt by the implied doubt of his linguistic capacity. "Vod can I do for zu; vould you like a baper?"

"No, I thank you, I bought one at the station. I beg pardon for troubling you, but can you tell me, please, if Mr. Vernon Corfe is here?"

"I do not think he is; he does not call every day."   •

"Then he does live here?—he is in Geneva now? He—I can—" she exclaims eagerly, almost breathlessly, and then comes to a full stop.

"Yes, he does live here; he is in Geneva," answers the German stolidly, but staring at her wonderingly. "Vod zu like me to shout up ze sbout and ask if he is in ze sub-editor's room? He is sometimes."

"Thank you very much, please do," returns the lady; on which the German goes a few yards away and applies his hairy mouth to what he called the "sbout." "I do hope he is not in, though," she murmurs, with trembling lips; "it would not be nice to meet him here before so many people."

By this time all the clerks are staring at her.

"No, he is not ub-stairs, Madame," says the German, returning from his excursion to the spout. "Can I do anything else for zu, Madame?"

"Thank you very much. If you could give me Mr. Corfe's private address I should be much obliged. The fact is, I omitted to write to him, or he would have met me at the station."

"I am sure he vod have done—anybody vod have done," answers the youth gallantly. "I do not know Mr. Corfe's brivat address, but I can get it for you in a wink."

As he speaks he goes away to the other end of the office, and in about five minutes comes back with a piece of paper, which he hands to the lady. On it are written the words, " Chez Madame Marcquart, rue du Chat Rouge 17, au troisième."

" If you will show this to the *cocher*," says the polite German, "he will take you direct to M. Corfe's lodgings."

The rue du Chat Rouge was some distance away, on the other side of the river. It ran at right angles to a main thoroughfare, and though the buildings were ancient and lofty, they were not inhabited by old or high-class families. The house before which the carriage stopped was large, slab-sided, and pierced by a large archway. The ground-floor rooms were used as shops ; one was a café ; the upper floors were dwellings, and as largely populated as a small cotton factory in full work.

" *Au troisième*," says the *cocher*, pointing upwards, "that is very high ; shall I mount your box ? "

The lady nods assent, whereupon the man, shouldering the trunk, precedes her up a wide stone staircase, the worse for wear, and neither very clean nor very well-lighted. There are two doors on every landing, and on reaching the third the *cocher* deposits the trunk before a door which, as a brass-plate over the bell-handle denotes, belongs to Madame Marcquart. Then, opening his right hand, and holding up his left with finger and thumb outspread, he says in a hoarse whisper :

"*Cinq francs, madame; je demande cinq francs.*"

"*Trop,*" answers the lady; and compressing her lips firmly, and putting on a resolute look, she lays three francs on his extended palm.

"Not at all," returns the man, breathing defiance and absinthe, and then, firing off a volley of *sacrés,* he points to the big box.

This appeal produces a fourth franc in coin, and "Not another penny!" in words, whereupon the driver, who, though he understands them not, understands the gesture by which they are accompanied, pockets his money and goes away sorrowful, for he has got only double his legal fare.

When Madame Marcquart, a tall, dark-visaged woman of a certain age, found at her door a young lady, with a big box, who asked for Mr. Corfe, she looked very much surprised, and answered that he was not in.

"*Je l'attendrai.* I am a near relative, and have come from England to see him," said the stranger, slowly and hesitatingly, as if she had got off the sentence by heart; and without waiting for Madame Marcquart's answer, she backed into the corridor, dragging after her the box.

Madame eyed this proceeding askance, and looked as if she thought her visitor more free than welcome; but instinctive courtesy overcoming momentary distrust, she opened the door of her *salon* and invited the owner of the box to give herself the trouble to enter.

The room was comfortable and much better furnished than, from the outside appearance of the building and the condition of the staircase, might have seemed likely. The floor was highly polished ; there were two or three fauteuils ; a vase of fresh flowers adorned the old-fashioned table, and the window commanded a fine view—over chimney tops—of lake, mountain, and forest.

" At last ! " moaned the new comer as, with a deep sigh, she sank into one of the fauteuils.

" *La pauvre petite!* " exclaimed Madame Marcquart, compassionately, as she looked on her visitor's weary face and dusty dress. " Madame must be very tired—she has travelled far. Shall I get her a cup of tea ? "

M. Corfe's near relative bowed her head in token of grateful acquiescence, and then, leaning back in the fauteuil, closed her eyes.

When her hostess returned with the tea, the stranger inquired, in set phrase, as if she had learnt it out of a conversation book, how soon M. Corfe would be in ? Madame Marcquart was not at all sure. It might be soon, it might not be soon. When M. Corfe had writing to do, he often came in about this time ; when he had not writing to do he was generally very late. He had been her lodger only a week or two. She had no other lodger. This was her salon, but she allowed M. Corfe, when she had not need of it herself, to use it as his workroom. That was his *sousmain* on the table. M. Corfe was very *gentil*, she liked him much, and he spoke French extremely well, almost without accent. His chamber was there, on the other side of the passage ; would Madame like to go in and arrange herself before he came ?

Of this offer the young woman gladly availed herself, and after a while came out of the chamber feeling very much better, and looking, as Madame Marcquart put it to her solitary domestic, " altogether ravishing." Then, resuming her seat on the fauteuil, she tried to brave herself for the coming struggle, and listened with beating heart for the footstep which should announce the arrival of Vernon Corfe. But she had been travelling for twenty-four hours, her eyes were heavy, and after an hour of strained expectation she fell into a doze from which she was roused by a sound of voices in the corridor.

Madame Marcquart was telling Corfe that somebody waited for him in the salon.

" Who is it ? " he asked carelessly.

" Go in, and you will see."

The next moment the door opens, the stranger rises from her fauteuil, and the two are face to face.

If he had beheld a ghost, Corfe could not have

been more surprised, and he would much rather
have seen ten ghosts than this woman of flesh and
blood.

"Oh, Vernon!" she exclaims, stretching out her
hands beseechingly towards him, "At last!"

"D—n you! What fiend sent you here?" he
hisses fiercely, his eyes gleaming savagely and his
face purpling with rage.

"Vernon, Vernon! you will break my heart. Oh,
this is a cold welcome after so long a separation,"
and the poor thing presses her hands wildly to her
head and the tears start to her eyes.

"Serve you right. I did not ask you to come.
Why the devil have you come?"

"Out of love for you. For, oh! in spite of all
that has passed, I love you still; I love you with all
my heart, Vernon!"

"That's all stuff! Anyhow you will have to go
back. I cannot do with you here."

"I shall never go back alive, Vernon," she
answers, looking strangely into his eyes, which
lower before hers. "You may desert me, as you
have done before, but I shall never desert you."

"But I will make you go; do you hear? I will
make you go," and he raises his hand menacingly,
as if he were minded to put his threat into instant
execution.

"Oh, no, Vernon, you don't mean that! You
cannot turn your wife from your door."

" You are not my wife."

" In the sight of God I am!."

" I don't know anything about God. But you
are not my wife in the sight of man, and that is all
I care for. Will you go, I ask again, or shall I
make you ? "

" No, I will not go! and you shall not make
me!" she cries, raising herself to her full height,
and eyeing him almost with scorn. " I am a fool; I
know, for caring for you—for pleading here for the
love you once vowed to cherish for me all your life.
But there are limits even to my endurance. Dare
to send me away, and I will tell everything. I will
go to the British consul, the British chaplain, and
the editor of the *Helvetic News*. They shall see my
marriage lines, and know who you are and what
you have done. How will that suit you,
Vernon ? "

And then, with head thrown defiantly back, she
paused for a reply. A great many thoughts passed
through Corfe's mind just then. He was wild with
rage at the shattering of his scheme to marry Vera
Leonino ; but to let Esther carry out her threat
would be worse still—he should lose all his engagements ; Geneva would be too hot to hold him.
Whatever happened there must be no exposure, and
perhaps—who could tell ?—there might still be a
chance. And Esther, her cheeks flushed and her
eyes bright with excitement, looked deuced pretty,

almost as pretty as she looked the first time he saw her in the goldsmith's shop at York.

"Can it be true—can you really, after all that has passed, still love me, Esther?"

"Some natures love only once, Vernon, and they love for ever. Mine is one of them. Even when they hate they love, and I felt just now as if I could hate you. It is cruel—cruel—to threaten to send me away."

"Do you believe I could, Esther—that I was in earnest?"

This in a voice so changed, so soft and caressing, that it seemed hardly possible it could be that of the man who a moment before had so brutally repulsed her. But Corfe understood women, and the pluck with which Esther had met his menaces, her beauty and her distress were rekindling his passion, if they had not touched his heart.

"You looked as if you were in earnest," she answers hesitatingly, "and I did think you meant it."

"No, I did not. I spoke to you like a brute, I know. But I could not believe that you still loved me. I thought you had come to annoy me, reproach me, and perhaps to importune me for money, and I lost my temper, for I am very poor. Esther!"

"Yes, Vernon."

"Can you forgive me? You are a good

woman, and I am a very bad man, and I have treated you abominably. But, if you will give me another chance, I will try to love you as I did long ago. Will you?"

And then he draws her to him, kisses her fondly, and she, throwing her arms round his neck, lays her head on his shoulder and weeps. Her foolish woman's heart is won once more, and, forgetful of her sufferings and his perfidy, she feels that she loves him as much as ever.

"We shall be married over again, shall we not, Vernon?" she murmurs, looking up at him through her tears; "so that it may be quite—quite legal, you know."

"Nay, that would never do, Esther. I can only account for your presence here by saying that we are married, and that family circumstances compelled us to separate for a time. But don't you see that to be married afresh would be equal to saying we were never married before? Some time, perhaps, but it cannot be done now."

"Well, never mind. If you'll be kind to me, I don't much care, and if anybody says anything, I can show my marriage lines. And, Vernon——" looking up at him archly.

"Yes, Esther, what is it?"

"You said just now you were poor."

"So I am. I have only what I make by giving lessons and writing for the *Helvetic*. When I earn eighty or a hundred francs in a week, I consider myself very fortunate."

"Well, I will help you; I can give lessons, too. I do not mean to be a burden to you. I ask only your love; can you give it me?"

"I think so. Now I have you in my arms all the old feeling seems to be coming back. Yes, I can love you" (kissing her) "but you must not tell any tales, you know."

"Trust me for that. Fancy a wife telling tales about her husband. And, Vernon——"

"Yes, Esther, what is it now?"

"I have some money."

"Ah!"

"Yes, five hundred pounds."

"Five hundred pounds! Where the deuce did you get it?"

"I will tell you. When we were married, or when I supposed we were, my father, as you know, cast me off altogether, and said he would never see me again, and I knew he would be as good as his word; and when you so cruelly left me——"

"I was obliged. They threatened to prosecute me," interposed Corfe sharply.

"But you might have let me know where you were. However, I will neither reproach you nor rake up unpleasant memories. I was going to say that after you left me I was obliged to earn my own living. I might have given lessons in music and painting, but I could not afford to wait for pupils, so I took to dressmaking, and being a good cutter-out, I did pretty well, though I could not save much. I was always wondering where you were, and I waited and longed for news of you until I almost fretted myself to death, and then my Aunt Ruth died, and, to my great surprise, left me five hundred pounds, and almost at the same time I heard that Mr. Josephs—he was my aunt's solicitor—had heard that you were at Geneva, doing something for the *Helvetic News*, so I came."

"So you came; and how did you find out this place ?"

"By calling at the office of the paper and asking for your address."

"The deuce you did! And what have you done with your fortune ?"

"Brought it with me. Here it is," taking from the inside of her dress a roll of notes and handing it to him.

"You don't mean — you cannot — all this money !"

"I mean to give it all to you, dear Vernon, and I wish I could give you as much every year—yes, every day."

Corfe was visibly touched; his lips trembled, and drawing the girl closer to him, he kissed her passionately.

"Jewess though you are, Esther, you are the

best Christian I ever knew. You do return good for evil, and no mistake. You are an angel, and I am—well, the other thing."

"No, no; don't say that, Vernon. I will not let even you slander my husband. There is room for improvement, perhaps, and I shall try to improve you; but you are not the other thing, not by any means, *mon mari*—that is proper French, isn't it? And if you were a very, very good man there would be no merit in loving you, would there, now? As for me being an angel, *nous verrons*."

"Not a bit of it. You are one, and of a good sort, too. Anybody who thinks differently had better not say so to me."

As Corfe spoke he put the notes into his pocket, and a spasm of disappointment darkened his face, for the thought crossed his mind, "What are these compared to two millions?"

But Esther saw not this portentous sign, and if she had seen it, might not have guessed its cause, or known how ominous it was of evil.

END OF VOLUME I.